Totally Bound Publishing books by Zelah Roberts

Single Books
Midsummer Man

I0571295

MIDSUMMER MAN

ZELAH ROBERTS

Midsummer Man
ISBN # 978-1-83943-992-6
©Copyright Zelah Roberts 2021
Cover Art by Louisa Maggio ©Copyright June 2021
Interior text design by Claire Siemaszkiewicz
Totally Bound Publishing

MIDSUMMER MAN

Chapter One

Renwick Castle stood high on the hill above the Wyvern Valley, its tranquil beauty bestowing an elegant timelessness upon the idyllic landscape of rolling cornfields and quaint villages below. Gilded flags fluttered from crenelated battlements in the golden afternoon sun and the vibrant ruby, emerald and sapphire stained-glass windows glowed like jewels, refracting dancing rainbows onto ancient stone floors. In the courtyard of the ancient keep, the blush-pink petals of apple blossom trees, caressed from their branches by the breeze, danced on the warm summer air like confetti.

In the grand ballroom of the castle, now an extremely elegant five-star hotel, two women, Holly Mason and Melissa Turner, were working in parallel, placing perfumed rose-pink charity auction lists and donation envelopes on tables already festooned with glittering silverware and sparkling candelabras entwined with ivy and white roses.

Tonight was a night they had been working towards for months. It was the night upon which all their hopes as the trustees of the charity 'Help the Homeless', rested — the night when most of the funds the charity needed for the coming year would be raised. Tonight was the night of the Help the Homeless Midsummer Ball.

Holly set down yet another envelope, then glanced up as her friend Melissa cleared her throat. "So," Melissa asked, "did you try the rose-petal bath-pourri, then?"

Holly looked at her friend curiously. Melissa had given her the lovely bath set for her birthday, with strict and rather mysterious instructions that she should use it the night before the ball. "I did," she confirmed, "as instructed. It was absolutely fabulous. The rose petals were floating on the water and the scent was out of this world. But I still don't understand why I had to use it last night, exactly."

Melissa looked smug. "I knew you'd do it. I bet Simon a jasmine-scented back massage that you would."

Holly choked back a laugh. Her recently married friend was still in the honeymoon phase of her relationship with her beloved Simon. "Why jasmine, specifically?"

"Holly! Don't you know that jasmine is supposed to stimulate your libido?"

"Ah- no. Can't say that I did. But really... Your libido needs stimulating?"

Melissa gave her a sheepish look. "Well, no. In all honesty, if it got any more stimulated, I'd probably die. But what a way to go!"

Holly rolled her eyes. Her friend was incorrigible. "Well, naturally I'm delighted to have earned you a jasmine-scented back rub, but you still haven't told me why I had to use my bubble bath last night."

They moved to another table and began distributing auction lists. "Ah, yes...that. Well, this castle has been here nearly a thousand years. And for every single one of them, it has celebrated the magic of midsummer, the longest day of the year and the time when the veil between this world and the next is at its thinnest."

"Uh-huh."

Melissa threw out a dramatic arm. "Powerful forces are abroad on midsummer's night. And in this castle, they are amplified — soaked into the very fabric of this building."

"Is that right?"

"Oh, believe me. It is."

"So, what do these powerful forces want with me, pray tell?"

Melissa looked at her triumphantly. "Well, you sprinkled rose-petals last night, didn't you?"

"Yes—"

"Well, the legend says that if you sprinkle rose petals on Midsummer's Eve, you'll meet the man of your dreams the next night. And that means, you'll meet him tonight!"

Holly put down her envelopes and looked at her friend in frank disbelief. "Really? The man of my dreams? It's going to bring to life Jamie from *Outlander*, is it?"

Melissa rolled her eyes. "There are good men in the real world, too, you know."

Holly shook her head, amused. In her considered opinion, the only good men were fictional ones. "Melissa, you know I love you," she began, wryly, "but I don't want a man. I like my life the way it is."

Damn right she did. She'd worked hard to get to where she was today, and now she was reaping the rewards of her labours. Her life was safe, settled and interesting, exactly the way she liked it. The last thing she wanted was some wretched man messing it all up.

Melissa looked at her sympathetically. "Holly, I know you had that awful stalker a couple of years ago. But you can't judge all men by one obsessive fan."

"Of course not."

"And I know Taylor wasn't the best boyfriend you could have wished for. You were just unlucky he turned out to be such an absolute —"

Holly raised a hasty hand. "I know. They're not all like him. Some of them are worse!"

"Oh, Holly, come on. That's not fair! Look at Simon."

It was true. Her friend really had found one of those mythical creatures — a good man. Mild-mannered, gentle and fathoms deep in love with his adorable wife, Simon was a gentleman of the first order. But a man like that would never want a woman as hard as she was, with a background like hers. "Okay, okay. I know. Granted, your Simon is lovely, and I'm sure there are other wonderful men out there — but not for me. I'm not in the market for any midsummer magic."

For a moment, a wispy cloud drifted over the sun and the room shadowed. Holly set down another auction list with careful precision. "Anyway, I'm too busy. I'm up to my neck in work."

"Work won't keep you warm at night. You won't get to the end of your life and wish you'd done more *work*."

Holly looked drily at her friend. "I won't get to the end of my life and wish I'd done more *men*, either."

"Oh, honestly, Holly —"

At that moment, Melissa's phone beeped, signalling a text message. Melissa glanced at the screen and a delighted smile spread over her face.

"It's Sadika. You'll never guess who she's just sold a last-minute ticket to?"

"Who?"

"Sir Mac Sinclair!"

Holly raised her eyebrows. Sir Mac Sinclair was known to practically anyone with a pulse in the UK, even her, and she was no follower of the lives of the rich and famous. As the billionaire owner of one of the most prestigious building companies in the country, he was lauded for successfully and sympathetically restoring some of Britain's most valuable and beloved historic buildings. As a qualified architect, he had also created some new structures which, with their fluid, sensuous silhouettes and environmentally friendly designs, were now considered modern classics. But he was also infamous for his obsessive need for privacy. He rarely appeared in public and declined all television interviews, which made it all the more surprising that he was coming to such a high-profile event.

Not only that, but tickets for the ball had sold out months ago, and he must have paid through the nose to get hold of one at the last minute. Sadika, who was responsible for selling tickets and organising the seating plan, must be tearing her hair out trying to slot him in at one of the tables.

Holly scowled. Although she was pleased that the charity had received more money, she hated the fact that the rich could have it all their own way, could casually buy into an event at the last minute without a by-your-leave.

"Well, great. That should get us some more publicity. Hopefully, he'll spend a fortune and we'll all be happy."

"True." Melissa's voice filled with excitement. "But more than that, this guy is hot. I mean, seriously *hot*. Oh, he'd be perfect for you!"

"Oh, right. Because I'm so hot myself."

"You are!" Melissa clapped her hands together, her eyes speculative. "You'd make the most amazing couple—"

"Oh, don't do me any favours. The last thing I need is some arrogant megalomaniac billionaire who loves nothing more than his own reflection!"

Melissa's face softened. "Give in, Holly. It's fate. You've sprinkled the rose petals, so you might as well accept it. True love's a comin' for you."

Holly shook her head. "No. No way. You know what the difference between true love and herpes is, right?"

"No..."

"Herpes lasts forever."

* * * *

Later that evening she sat in that same ballroom with its fabulous, stuccoed ceiling and fruit trees adorned with white lights at every mullioned window. She was dressed in a slender silver ballgown that shimmered in the candlelight, her chestnut hair in an artful topknot, and waited to be called up to the charity auction by the compere, Jack De Vere.

Her stomach was in knots at the thought of going up on the stage, and at that moment, she half-wished she'd never had that fateful conversation with Melissa just before Christmas six months previously.

She'd been deeply mired in the plot of her seventh *Wayfarer Chronicles* book when her friend had called round.

'*So, how's the writing going?*' Melissa had asked, casually.

'*Not bad,*' Holly had told her, as they'd sat drinking coffee in the warm, cosy kitchen. Outside, snow had been falling in soft, dreamy drifts, covering the lawn and the overhanging trees with a delicate, satin-smooth mantle. "*Drake and Isabella are now on board a pirate ship bound for the West Indies. When they get there, she's going to be kidnapped and Drake's going to go after her with the help of a disgraced English captain and a servant girl who turns out to be a runaway heiress. But in the meantime, Isabella is going to escape with the help of two slaves...*"

Melissa had shaken her head in disbelief. '*I don't know how you do it,*' she'd said. '*All those characters... How on earth do you keep up with them all?*'

'*It's easy. The characters are real to me, so real that I wouldn't be at all surprised if Drake walked through that door right now...*'

'*Oh, I wish,*' Melissa had replied so fervently that Holly laughed. Drake was such a swoon-worthy hero that fans had created a Facebook fan page devoted to him, and Holly regularly received requests for details such as his birthday, his favourite food and his sexual position of choice. Such questions had increased in volume exponentially over the last year as the first of her books had been televised, to great acclaim. Her book sales had rocketed, and there was talk of reissuing some of her earlier stories. Her publishing company, recognising that they had a major coup on their hands, had even ended up licensing the rights to create merchandise around the stories, and the first mugs, coasters, notebooks, pens and candles were already on the shelves.

'*You know,*' Melissa had said slowly, '*have you ever considered auctioning off a character in one of your books?*'

Holly had looked at her quizzically. '*What do you mean?*'

'*I mean, offer to name a character in one of your books after the auction winner. That definitely would be a prize that money couldn't buy!*'

'*You really think that would fly?*' she'd asked doubtfully.

Melissa had clasped a dramatic hand to her forehead. '*You bet your bottom dollar I do! I bet there are millions of fans out there who'd give an arm and a leg to be immortalised alongside Drake and Isabella. And the publicity for an auction lot like that would be through the roof! Can you imagine? Everyone would know about the Midsummer Ball and Help the Homeless!*'

Her friend had been absolutely right. In fact, the subsequent furore had been greater than either of them could ever have imagined. Holly had been invited onto radio and television shows to discuss the auction and the charity. Newspapers, magazines and websites had run articles, and one mega-famous film star had been quoted as saying he would give his left testicle to be featured in a *Wayfarer Chronicle*. Holly had wondered cynically how much he considered his left testicle to be worth, but she had noticed that he was on the list of ticket holders for tonight. Hopefully, he'd put his money where his…mouth was.

The trustees had decided to leave her auction lot as the grand finale, and Jack, the compere, was currently working his way through the others. The auction publicity had prompted several well-known companies and public figures to offer donations, and so it was possible to bid on all sorts of items, including a week for two on a luxury yacht in the Bahamas, a signed football from a world-famous team and executive tickets with a backstage pass to a sold-out tour of a famous British boy-band.

The atmosphere was electric as Jack joked and cajoled his ebullient audience into higher and higher bids. Every winning bid drew a round of laughter and applause. The champagne had flowed with abandon since the event had begun and had been followed by a delicious summery meal featuring fresh salmon and strawberries.

"Now come on, ladies. This fabulous pure silk Hermès scarf is named after the messenger of the gods...and you'll look like a goddess wearing it, especially if you're wearing nothing else. Gentlemen, take note. Give your lady a delivery she'll never forget!"

Holly suppressed a wince, hoping she would not be the target of any equally smutty innuendos. But given that her books did involve some powerful sex scenes, she thought it unlikely that the compere would be able to resist the temptation.

"The lovely lady with the excellent taste at the back, six hundred... Do I hear seven...?"

"I think that man was a pirate in a previous life."

The rich masculine voice, with the deep consistency of rich, dark molasses, disturbed Holly's concentration. She turned in time to see a man slide into the seat next to her.

Her mouth dropped open. *Drake!*

She had told the truth to Melissa. Her characters were real to her, but they weren't *actually* real. She definitely didn't expect a man who was the perfect embodiment of her male hero to sit down beside her.

For a moment, her world seemed to tilt. Was this some sick cosmic joke? Something she had dreamed up as a result of her conversation with Melissa earlier? Was this her midsummer man, invoked by superstition and a fragrant handful of rose petals? Was she going completely mad?

He grinned at her, his laughing, sapphire-blue eyes intelligent and teasing in a face that was quite simply the most handsome example of the male species she had ever seen.

Her gaze drifted down the long length of him. Quite apart from his startling and gorgeous face, his body was just ridiculous.

Ridiculously sexy, anyway. The man's shoulders were wide and muscular, his arms beneath the elegant tuxedo jacket evidently strong and powerful. His chest was broad, his torso slim, his legs, encased in well-cut black trousers, muscular. Even his feet, shod in expensive polished black leather, were sexy.

And his scent. Good grief, she'd never smelt anything like it in her life. It was like cedar with a faint hint of lemon, reminding her randomly and vividly of a sunlit woodland. Beneath it there was a faint warm muskiness, the scent of clean, healthy male. It was delicious.

Holly, who had never in her life even thought about the appeal of a man's scent before, reacted in a sudden, wholly feminine way that brought a flush of heat to her cheeks.

Which was *so* not needed right now. She had to pull herself together. What on earth was the matter with her? He was just a man, an ordinary man — nothing at all to do with Melissa's arrant, superstitious nonsense. Snapping to attention and hoping he hadn't noticed her rather intent appraisal of him, she cleared her throat.

"Yes," she said, huskily. "he's definitely doing his job. I can't believe how much that scarf is going for."

She watched, bemused, as a complacent, well-preserved man in his sixties waved his programme.

"Nine hundred…"

"Crazy," she breathed.

"No." Drake, as she'd dubbed him, made a subtle gesture towards the pretty young woman clad in a daringly skimpy black dress who sat beside the older man. "He's making a statement. Showing the girl he's trying to impress that he's got the power to lavish money around for the right inducement."

"Cynical."

He shrugged. "Not me. Just realistic. Beauty and power… They always come together."

She glanced at him, her writer's mind wondering if the pun was intentional. He smiled at her blandly.

"And now, ladies and gentlemen, the one you've all been waiting for. Tonight, the woman who created the dark, delicious and debonair Drake Blaine and the feisty, fiery, flirtatious firebrand Isabella Heron is here to offer a once-in-a-lifetime opportunity—" he broke off as the crowd clapped, whistling and cheering.

Holly swallowed, feeling sick. She'd never aspired to the stage, and, quite frankly, she dreaded going up there. Drake leaned over to whisper in her ear. "You look like you're going to the gallows. Courage, now. And afterwards, will you dance with me?"

She looked into his beautiful eyes, and suddenly all her nerves were forgotten—which, she realised, was what he'd probably intended. She shot him a quick grin. "Depends how much you bid," she said teasingly.

"So, ladies and gentlemen, with no more ado, allow me to give you a taste of the beautiful, the adventurous, the wild and wicked…Holly Mason!"

A huge round of applause thundered through the room. Like an automaton, she mounted the steps and prayed she wouldn't send herself flying on her spindly silver heels. Making it to the top, she turned to face the audience. The electric sense of expectation and anticipation in the ballroom was acute. She really needed to put on her game face and brazen this out.

With a wide, sassy grin, she waved at the audience and blew them a kiss. There was a roar of approval and some enthusiastic wolf whistles.

Wrapping an unwelcomed arm around her, the rather sweaty Jack smiled genially at the crowd. "Well, now, Isabella," he began, and ripple of laughter ran through the room. "Oh, I'm sorry... *Holly*. But, boys, don't you think she looks just like the glorious Isabella Heron with her fantastic shapely...gown and beautiful bedroom hair?"

For a moment, Holly just stared at him, unable to believe his blatant sexism and crassness. The temptation to tell him to take a running jump was overwhelming. But then common sense prevailed. She would have that discussion with him in private, after she had charmed the audience into bidding on her lot. So instead, she just contented herself by purring, "Why, thank you... You'll forgive me if I don't call you Drake with your...ah... figure..." She nodded at his portly frame, noting with satisfaction that his smile slipped a bit, "and your beautiful... ah..." She let her voice trail off a bit whilst inclining her head subtly towards his. Far from having 'bedroom hair', he had no hair at all. She smiled cheekily at the audience, who collapsed into laughter and applause.

Less than five minutes later, the ballroom was silent and tense as the bidding narrowed to two competing parties. She could see one of them from where she was stood — the actor. She heartily hoped he wouldn't win. She would have the devil's own job getting the name 'Woody Savage' into one of her novels.

"Five hundred thousand pounds."

"Six…"

The bidding crept up in ones, neither bidder willing to lose the prize. Holly held her breath. She had never imagined it would go so high. Even Jack was sounding a bit strangled.

Then, from the deep shadows at the side of the stage, a familiar voice drawled, "Two million, if it comes with a dance with the lady."

Drake. Drake had bid *two million pounds.* Who on earth was he to be able to throw vast sums of money around like that? And who did he think he was, trying to buy a dance with her?

An audible, collective gasp came from the audience. Stunned and defeated, the other bidders shook their heads immediately.

Jack glanced at Holly, seeking confirmation of the dance. Reluctantly, she nodded. After all, she could hardly refuse that kind of money for Help the Homeless just because she didn't like being manipulated by rich, powerful men who thought they could buy anything they wanted.

"Two million pounds, ladies and gentlemen. Two million! Do we have any advance on two million?"

Silence. Even from the world-famous actor, who was scowling into his drink and looking decidedly disgruntled.

"Okay, if we're all done… To the gentleman on my left…going, going, *gone!*"

There was a round of rapturous applause as Drake came up onto the stage. Once again she was struck by how unbelievably gorgeous and charismatic he was. In his beautifully cut tuxedo, he looked lean, strong and powerful.

Powerful enough to have forced her into a dance. Her stomach twisted uncomfortably. She hated the fact that he had been able to compel her to do what he wished, even in so small a way.

But she hated even more how she reacted to him. Of course, she'd been attracted to men in the past, but she'd never met anyone who had caused quite such an immediate, visceral, physical impact. Was it because he reminded her of her beloved Drake?

It seemed unlikely. The man who stood before her was a living, breathing, all-too-real human, his physicality a powerful part of what was drawing her to him. He made her want to be close to him, even as she wanted to run from the intense emotions that he was arousing in her.

And she sure didn't like his ability to spend millions of pounds on a frivolous auction. That meant he had serious fiscal power — and she really didn't like rich men. In her experience, they were self-absorbed, morally corrupt and dangerous.

She caught him looking at her and veiled her dark expression from his curious, perceptive eyes. He stepped forward and held out his hand to shake hers.

Aware of the audience watching, she reluctantly put her hand in his. "Miss Mason, it's a pleasure to meet you," he said. To her dismay, his big hand engulfed hers, the contact of skin against skin making her shiver inside. His grasp was warm, firm, strong. She could almost imagine the surprisingly rough skin of his hands stroking against more sensitive skin, bringing untold pleasure.

Quashing the thought, she smiled politely at him. "The pleasure is mine, Mr. — ?"

"Sinclair. Mac Sinclair."

A ripple of interest ran through the audience. Almost as one, they reached for their mobile phones, and Holly was acutely aware that in the next few minutes photos of them both would be appearing all over social media. Not that it seemed to bother him. He looked remarkably sanguine in the limelight—much more relaxed than she herself felt, truth be told, though she hoped she appeared at ease.

As if he somehow understood her feelings, he gave her hand a subtle, reassuring squeeze. And as she looked up at him, all she could think was that Melissa had been right. Mr. Rich-and-Famous was *hot*. And it was surely a sign of how rattled she was, she thought, that she would resort to such a lame, completely inadequate adjective to describe him.

Jack cleared his throat. "Well, ladies and gentlemen, I give you Sir Mac Sinclair. How do you feel, Sir Mac, to have won such a fabulous prize?"

He smiled out over the audience. "Just Mac, please. I'm delighted, of course. Thrilled. And very grateful to Miss Mason for offering such a fabulous prize in support of Help the Homeless."

"Indeed. And for you, it will be a wonderful thing to be featured in such a fabulous series."

Mac shook his head. "Oh, no. Not me. I'm hoping that Miss Mason will be kind enough to include my sister's name in her next book. This is a gift for her. She—and I—are huge fans of the *Wayfarer* series."

"Your sister?" Jack exclaimed. "What's her name?"

"It's Leonie," he said. "Leonie Sinclair."

"Well, there you have it," said Jack, turning to the audience. "Ladies and gentlemen, you heard it here first. Leonie Sinclair...the newest character in the *Wayfarer* series!"

* * * *

Afterwards, there was dancing, and Holly looked at him mutinously when he held out his hand to her. He lowered it, warily. "I've annoyed you?"

Her temper sparked. "No. Of course not. Why would I be annoyed at being coerced and manipulated into doing something I don't want to do?"

He stepped back immediately. "My apologies," he said, stiffly. "I didn't intend for one moment to make you feel that you *had* to dance with me. I never have, and never will, force a woman to do anything against her will. Now, if you'll excuse me."

He turned and walked away, his rigid back reflecting his displeasure. Holly swore beneath her breath. Now *she* felt guilty. To be fair, he had asked her for a dance before the bidding. And *she* had jokingly suggested the idea of payment.

Damn, damn, damn... She was an idiot.

Her conscience was not going to let her off the hook. She owed him an apology.

Before she could agonise anymore, she set off after him. "Dra— Mac, wait," she called.

He stopped, turned. "Did you just start to call me *Drake*?"

She shrugged. "Slip of the tongue."

"Uh-huh." He stood, his arms folded, and waited for her to speak. He looked brooding, formidable and unyielding.

"I owe you an apology," she blurted out.

He raised an eyebrow. "No. Really? Why?"

His sarcasm made her wince, but she squared her shoulders. "I shouldn't have gone off at you about the dance. You asked me before the auction, and it was me who suggested bidding on it...as a joke, of course."

"Of course. Which was how I meant it, as well."

His tone was frosty.

"Ah...yes. So, I'm sorry. Okay."

She turned to go, but a hand on her arm stopped her. "Why, Holly?" he asked, his voice deep and gravelly.

"Why what?"

"Why did you 'go off at me,' as you put it?"

"Oh." She bit her lip and looked away from his probing gaze. "I'm a bit sensitive about being manipulated. I don't like it when I feel trapped or pushed into things."

"I see. So, will you feel pushed into it if I ask you to dance now? For free, this time?"

She looked up at his glittering eyes, which now glimmered with mischief, and she smiled. *What the hell.* She might be wary of alpha males in general, but there was no harm in enjoying a dance with one...especially one she was so very attracted to. It wasn't as if she were offering to have his babies, after all.

"Well, since you've asked so nicely..."

His lips quirked. "I can ask extremely nicely when the need arises," he murmured, and a bubble of laughter welled up inside her.

The band was playing a lively number, the lead female vocalist belting it out with impressive verve. Soon, they were both dancing, swirling and moving in sync with the pulsing music and the coloured lights flashing across the dance floor. Holly found herself laughing out loud. Drake—no, *Mac*—was fun to dance with, maintaining eye contact and taking frequent opportunities to twirl her so that she found herself often in his strong arms or pressed against his lean, hard body. It was exhilarating.

She'd thought he'd stop after a while, head back to his table for a drink or offer to dance with someone else.

But he was indefatigable, and it became an unspoken game that neither of them would give in and stop dancing. She didn't want to anyway. She was enjoying herself too much.

Still, it was a relief for her feet when, towards the end of the set, a slow dance came on. With a wide, welcoming smile, he held his arms open to her, and she went into them.

Oh, the pleasure. He still smelt delicious, clean and masculine. He wrapped his arms around her and pressed his strong body firmly against hers. He was taut and muscular and felt wonderful. Holly's eyes fluttered closed as she rested her head against his broad shoulder and swayed along to the music.

She felt the soft touch of his lips on her hair and looked up into his brilliant blue eyes. They glittered with an unmistakeable intensity.

He took a ragged breath then muttered, "Damn, Holly…"

Pulling back a little, she looked keenly at him. "What is it?" she asked softly.

A dull flush ran across his high cheekbones. "I… When I came here tonight, I didn't imagine… I wish —"

He broke off.

"You wish what?"

He swallowed. "I wish that things were different. I'm no Prince Charming. There's no place in my life for a relationship, not even for a fling. But I wish… I wish I could have you, spend time with you tonight. A time out of time, just for us. I've truly never felt anything like this before…"

There was a long silence as Holly considered his words. She'd never felt anything like it either. And, goodness knew, she definitely wasn't in the market for a relationship, especially with a rich alpha male like this one. But one night, just for them... It sounded wonderful.

She wanted him more than she'd ever wanted anyone in her whole life. She'd never felt chemistry like it. This might be her only chance to ever have what she was sure would be a brilliant experience with someone who really 'did it' for her. She would be a fool to turn down such an opportunity.

She smiled slowly and took a deep breath. "You know, Mac, I don't need — or want — a prince. I have my own life, my own money and I don't need rescuing, thank you very much. But I am interested in interior décor."

"Interior décor?"

"Mmm. I hear the bedrooms in this castle have the most fabulous furnishings."

* * * *

They did. The room he took her to had a beautiful trefoil mullioned window with a soft, padded window seat. The walls were panelled in oak and hung with red and gold tapestries. But what drew the eye more than anything else was an exquisite, Tudor-style oak tester bed carved with vine leaves and grapes, which was laden with thick, sumptuous cushions.

"Oh, this *is* beautiful," Holly breathed, even as she tried to quell the unexpected butterflies in her stomach. Would she soon find herself entwined around him on that very bed?

It was memories of her ex-partner, Taylor, that were inhibiting her, she knew. He had been her first and only — a nice, non-alpha, anodyne kind of guy. She'd been attracted to him because he felt safe and mild and sensible. She'd needed that after all the instability and chaos of her young life.

Though, as time had passed, he had become more controlling, more jealous, more critical. When she had plucked up the courage to call a halt to their destructive relationship, he had been brutal in his condemnation. *'You're a frigid cow,'* he'd snarled at her. *'No man will ever want you. You're ugly and fat and you wouldn't know what to do with a man if he came with instructions. Pathetic!'*

She'd moved on since Taylor—Melissa and her other friends had helped her pick up the pieces. Nowadays she was much more confident and certain of herself, except in the bedroom. She'd never risked sex with anyone again…until now.

Granted, she hadn't met a single man who had made her even *want* to have sex. Mac, though, was different. Somehow, he had awakened all kinds of yearnings in her. Her body felt wild and restless and oddly *hungry*.

Mac watched her prowl tensely around the room. It didn't take a genius to see that she was nervous, though she was putting up a good front admiring the furnishings.

It surprised him how much he disliked seeing her so uneasy. He wouldn't want any woman to be uncomfortable in his presence, but he really, really hated seeing Holly like this. Downstairs she had been relaxed, laughing, full of effervescent joy. But now, she was a pale facsimile of herself.

How could he put her at ease? Keeping his body language relaxed, he said, "Would you like a drink?"

She glanced at him then away, folding her arms. "Ah, yes, please."

He went to the mini bar, which was concealed behind some panelling. "Okay, what would you like?

There are all the usual culprits in here, plus a few quirky extras. Or I could send down for some champagne?"

Holly smiled, shaking her head. "Quirky extras sound interesting. What have you got?"

She joined him, peering into the tiny fridge. At least she was willing to come near him.

"Lindisfarne mead," she read, pulling out a small bottle. "What is it?"

"Do you have a sweet tooth?"

"Mmm-hmm."

"You might like it then. It's a honey liqueur, originally brewed by monks…"

"You're kidding!"

"Nope. Try it."

He opened the little bottle and poured the golden liquid into a glass. She took a tentative sip. "Oh! That's delicious."

He laughed, selecting a whisky for himself. She looked at him curiously and he shook his head. "Too sweet for me."

"Ah."

"Come and sit on the window seat. The gardens are lit up at night. It's worth a look."

He switched the lights off so that the soft pastel lights in myriad colours glowed in the darkness. It was a beautiful, clear evening. A million stars were twinkling, and the warm breeze was little more than a soft breath. The branches of the nearby oaks, which must have been two hundred years old if they were a day, rippled gently as if stroked by a soft hand.

Holly and Mac sat at either end of the window seat with their drinks and looked out. "Put your legs up," Mac urged. "Take the weight off your feet." He looked down at her silver sandals. "Beautiful though these are, would you like to take them off?" he asked.

"Mmm. That sounds good."

It sounded good to him, too. That she was willing to take her shoes off told him that she wasn't immediately thinking of bolting on him, which was something.

He slid her shoes off and gently massaged a small, neat foot. She flinched imperceptibly. "You're very tense, sweetheart," he said, casually, stroking the soft skin of her sole. She had pretty toes. "You know you don't have to do this, don't you?"

She flushed. "Of course. I... I'm just a bit nervous."

"About what?"

There was a silence.

His mind raced. What the hell could be making her so twitchy?

The answer was obvious. He was an idiot. "Are you worried about precautions? Because I'll take care of that."

He always did. It was absolutely his responsibility to make sure they were both safeguarded.

"Oh! Ah, well, that would be good. Thanks."

But that evidently was not what was bothering her.

"Out with it," he said, gruffly. "You were like a flame in my arms downstairs, but now that we're here, you've dimmed to candlelight. What's bothering you?"

She looked away, awkwardly.

"Come on, sexy lady," he coaxed. "You were damn well brave enough to get up on that stage tonight with hundreds of people watching. I'm sure you can tell me what's on your mind."

She pulled her feet away from him and drew her knees up against her chest, wrapping her arms around herself. With visible difficulty, she admitted, "I...had a past relationship. This sort of thing...wasn't great."

The whisky in his glass glowed rich and tawny in the ambient light. He swirled it round absently, thinking about all she hadn't said. Had her previous lover been inconsiderate? Careless? Cruel?

A sudden tide of protectiveness swept over him, surprising him with its intensity. He had always been deeply protective of his family, but that feeling did not normally extend to near strangers. But for all that he'd only known Holly for one evening, she was no stranger to him. He felt, oddly, as if he'd known her for years, as if she were aligned with him, in tune with him in some deep, intimate way.

A prickle of unease made him shift uncomfortably. He liked women, enjoyed their company and their bodies on rare occasions, but he was not interested in getting involved with anyone. For one, he wasn't idiot enough to make himself vulnerable to a woman by loving her. He'd done that once. *Never again.* For another, he had more trouble and responsibilities on his plate at present than he could comfortably handle and had no wish to add any further upheaval to his life.

But even so, he could not subdue his instincts. He hated the thought that Holly might have been mistreated. He hated that she was nervous around him. He wanted to give her everything that it appeared she had been denied in the past. He wanted her to feel safe and cared for. He wanted her to know the power of passion and pleasure.

He looked at her with resolve. "I'm sorry it wasn't good for you. And I want you to know you'll not come to any harm with me. Your word is law, here. You say 'no', and it's 'no'…at any point. Do you understand me?"

She looked at him seriously. "I do," she said. "But I'm not going to say 'no'."

Thank goodness.

"And," he said, reflecting, "there's one other thing."

"What's that?"

"Tonight is our night. When I danced with you downstairs, I saw a woman who was vivid, beautiful, confident. And when you danced..." He rolled his eyes. "Holly, you were glorious. Absolutely, utterly sensual. And tonight, I want that woman with me. So I'm challenging you. Shake off the nerves, relax and let go. Tonight I want the open, honest, real you."

She raised an eyebrow. "You ask a lot, Sir Mac."

"Yep. I'm a demanding man, all right," he said easily.

"You might bite off more than you can chew."

"I'll risk it if you will."

There was a long pause. Then Holly said slowly, "Okay. But be prepared. When I take on a challenge, I do it right. And I'll only do it on one condition."

"What's that?"

"That you're equally open and honest with me. Let's see who you really are, Mac Sinclair. I dare you."

She surprised him by rummaging in her purse for her phone. A few seconds later, *Unchained Melody* was playing in the background.

She stood and held out her hand. "Dance with me," she said, softly. "You're right. Tonight is just for us. Just one secret, magical night. So tonight I'm going to be...who I want to be. Who I really am inside."

He nodded solemnly. "I want that. I want it so much, Holly. Something real. And I promise you that it'll be the real me. There'll only be truth between us."

A wicked, sinfully seductive smile spread across her face, and suddenly, instinctively, he knew he was seeing the real Holly, the one she hid from others. And she was magnificent—confident, powerful, strong, determined and wicked.

"Truth it is," she murmured, huskily.

His stomach clenched and the deep, dark excitement that had been brewing all evening coalesced into a burning coil of need in the pit of his stomach.

He put his hand into hers and found himself on his feet, in her arms, slow dancing in time with the music.

Oh, it was so wonderful to finally have her warm, lithe, sensuous body against his. With her feminine curves, her softness, against him, his breath hitched. She was a temptress, a witch. He was falling under her spell.

Her scent twined around him. She smelt faintly of roses. He pressed his face against the tender skin of her collar bone, breathed in the faint, delicious musk of her skin. His head spun. He was drowning in his need for her.

Unable to resist, he tasted her—clean, sweet, faintly salty. Lust hit him hard, squirming and writhing. What would it be like to taste her more intimately? Would she let him? To bathe in her scent, to feel her softness against his face, to see the beauty of her body...

As if bewitched, he sought out her mouth, unable to bear another second without a kiss. She opened to him and he stroked her lips with his. He had never done that before, never thought about the sheer, intimate, delicious sensation of mouth against mouth. Her lips were so soft, so smooth... Then she thrust her tongue into his mouth and he nearly came on the spot.

Gasping, breathing in her air, he submitted as she took him into her, her tongue toying with his, dancing and jousting. The tiny, soft jabs instantly had him imagining what it would be like to be inside her. Would her body be so hot, so soft, so welcoming?

He groaned, and suddenly she twisted in his arms, so that she was facing away from him. He kept his arms around her but could not resist sliding his hands across the plane of her stomach, the curve of her hips. She laughed softly, and pressed her bottom against him, gyrating against him in time with the music.

"Damn," he whispered hoarsely as more desire flooded his already-desperate body. Intense heat swept through him. He was on fire, and she was fanning the flames, over and over, rubbing and pressing against him.

He longed to seize her by the waist, bend her over, move aside her silky little panties and slip inside her soft warmth, lose himself in her... And she would groan and moan and push back against him until she tightened around him.

Swallowing hard, he fought for control, but his hazy mind could not resist temptation and he slid his hands to her delicious breasts in their sparkly covering. They filled his palms, two delicious little mounds.

She leaned forward and he stroked them softly, lightly. She gasped and shivered. The soft motion of her hips changed. His light caresses were obviously inflaming her.

She turned, a sultry smile that was pure delight playing on her lips.

Reaching out to the lapel of his jacket, she looked deeply into his eyes. "May I?" she asked, stroking the collar.

He nodded, helplessly, and she slid the jacket from his shoulders. His shirt came next. She unbuttoned it slowly, never dropping his gaze, and took it from him.

Her soft, slender hands slid over his sensitised skin and he shivered.

"Shoes off," she whispered.

He slipped them off with alacrity.

"Socks."

He glanced at her curiously then took them off. She wrinkled her nose. "I hate seeing a man wearing socks without trousers," she said. "It's not a good look."

He made a mental note of that for next time, then berated himself. There wasn't going to be a next time. Suddenly, he found himself hating that thought.

But there was no opportunity to ponder. Her hands at his belt obliterated every logical thought process he had left. She unfastened it efficiently, opened it and carefully slid down his zipper. He groaned as the constriction of his close-fitting dress trousers eased, then her hands were at his waistband and she was sliding both the trousers and his boxer shorts off him.

Gasping as she ran her hands over his bottom, he realised that she was slowly pushing the fabric past his hips. A second later, he sprang free as the trousers slid down his legs. The cool air stroked his heated body.

"Get on the bed," she whispered.

His eyes widened. He'd never had this before, never had a woman who had so completely taken charge. It was intensely erotic to cede control, to put himself in her hands. Truth, he had promised her, but he had not known this about himself, had not suspected he was capable of submission, even for a short time.

It turned him on like hell.

He stumbled to the bed.

"On your back," she said.

He lay back, realising that whilst he was stripped, she was fully clothed. The thought made him feel vulnerable.

Maybe she recognised a little of what he was feeling, because she crawled onto the bed beside him and kissed him. He brought his hands up to wrap around her body, but she caught his wrists and held them firm against the pillows until he obeyed and left them where they were. It was very frustrating only to be able to kiss her and not touch anywhere else, but hell, it was surely the best kiss of his life, bar none.

She pressed her lips to his and carried on kissing him until neither of them had breath, and still she kept going, until all was swirling colour and throbbing feeling. Only when his body was straining upwards, seeking touch, did she reach down and lightly stroke across his stomach.

His muscles contracted as he contorted into an arch, trying to manoeuvre the fingers to stroke lower, at his hips, his groin.

But they refused to go, instead stroking his underarm, his sides, his ribs. Once they brushed across a nipple, and he shuddered.

"Please," he gasped, groaning, and with a wicked little laugh, she reached down and pinched it, hard.

The pleasure-pain would have brought him to his knees if he'd been upright. As it was, it took him to the edge and he panted as those fingers, those wicked, damn, torturous fingers, drifted away once again and swirled around the tops of his legs, millimetres from his balls.

He thrust his hips in frustration. He was so hard and full and tight that he feared he might burst.

"Damn it, Holly," he ground out, "please!"

But she pressed a pretty pearl-pink polished fingertip to his lips, smiled and murmured, "Sshhh. Be good, now."

Be good?

It was nearly his undoing. She was driving him crazy. She was *killing* him...

He twisted and writhed as she stroked all around him, coming so close to touching him. He knew that was all it would take. He was on a knife edge.

"Please, Holly, please..." he begged, desperate for her to take pity on him. "Anything. Please..."

She laughed, *laughed*. Then slowly, she slid down his body and took him into her mouth.

The shock of it took his breath away. For a frozen second, he fought a pitched battle with his body. She drew him deep inside, and at the sudden sensation of enfolding heat, his control splintered. The impulse to thrust and thrust hard, to take, to find release was overwhelming. But he couldn't... He didn't want to.

He twisted away from her, hauled her up against him and kissed her with a fierce passion that left her wild and breathless.

"Why? Why did you stop?" she asked.

For a fleeting second, he thought he saw a shadow of doubt in her eyes. Did she seriously think he hadn't wanted to?

"I was too close," he whispered harshly. "You're a witch, an absolute bloody siren. A man could drown in passion for you..."

She flushed, and there was something new in her eyes, a dawning of new confidence. It filled him with satisfaction. Whoever her useless lover had been, he was a bloody idiot to let this woman go. She was pure, pure dynamite.

"You could have—"

"I want my first time with you to be...in you."

Her eyes widened, and he rolled over, pressing her down into the soft mattress. He touched the zip at the side of her dress.

"Sexy lady... May I?" he asked.

She laughed softly, nodded and wriggled to help him undo the zip and slide the silky material down.

He felt like he was unwrapping the most amazing present he had ever received.

And when her dress was finally off, he knelt beside her and just looked his fill.

She was, far and away, the most breathtakingly beautiful woman he had ever seen. In the soft light from the garden, she was all shadows and mysteries. He absorbed the vision of her slender neck, delicate collar bones and smooth, creamy alabaster shoulders. His gaze travelled downwards, down towards the promised land of her sweet, smooth, strawberry-tipped breasts, so perfect. He swallowed as he followed the slender plane of her stomach and her softly curved hips to the tiny panties he'd imagined, gorgeous little silky silver ones with an edging of lace. And finally to her legs—her long, long legs and dainty feet. She was so exquisite that he was almost afraid to touch her.

He breathed deeply, fighting to subdue his own needs so he could fulfil hers.

"You're perfect," he whispered. "Like a fairy or a fey. Magical."

She shook her head, met his eyes and looked deep into them. "Just a woman," she said.

"There's no 'just' about it."

He lay on his side beside her and reached out to stroke her breast. She tensed. "You don't like this?" he asked. "You have to tell me, you know. Anything you don't like…"

Her gaze slid away from his. "It hurts…"

He removed his hand immediately, frowning. "It hurts? When I touch you like that?"

Her colour was high, but she answered him. "Not now. But…later."

"Later?"

"You know. When things get a bit...wilder."

What the bloody hell? He bit off a sharp expletive as black fury roared through him. If he ever met this ex-lover, he'd want to kill him. It was obvious that the guy had been rough with her — too damn rough by far if she thought that normal lovemaking meant pain. No wonder she had been nervous.

It occurred to him that she had paid him the most enormous compliment by trusting him enough to come to bed with him.

He swallowed. He would make this good for her. At his hands, she would learn that lovemaking could be wonderful from beginning to end.

"There is no wilder," he murmured. "No damn wilder and no damn pain. I promise." He looked into her eyes. "Do you trust me, sweetheart?"

"Yes."

"Will you let me...try? To touch you *there*? It won't hurt, I promise. And if it does, just tell me to stop and I will. At any point. All right?"

There was apprehension in her eyes, but she nodded. "All right."

Breathing a sigh of relief, he kissed her, and kept on kissing her until the tension eased out of her. And he kept on kissing her as he began to stroke her breasts with a featherlight touch, circling gently, avoiding her beautiful nipples.

He took his time, letting his fingers drift, much as she had on him, until she started to move of her own accord. He smiled inwardly as he felt the first faint arching of her back, a sure sign that her breasts were seeking a firmer touch.

He didn't give it to her, continuing the slow torture until she started to moan and undulate her hips.

He breathed in deeply as he watched her sensuous movements. He could smell the delicious scent of her, and it made him dizzy. He wanted her so much.

Unable to help himself, he lowered his head to her breast and sucked softly. His stomach clenched at the soft, sweet taste of her skin, the feel of it against his lips. His breath caught as a wave of pleasure rolled over him.

She arched, crying out, even as he slid his hand down her body and between her legs. The silk of her panties was soaking. He stroked the damp, slick fabric as he licked and kissed her breasts, until she was squirming with need.

By then he was lost himself. Feeling the wet silk beneath his fingers slide over her softness had him on the rack. He wanted to replace his fingers with his mouth. He smelled her warm muskiness, but he wanted to taste her, to absorb her, to consume her.

Unable to resist, he slid down her body and farther still. Still caught in the moment, she let him, then suddenly seemed to realise what he was doing and jack-knifed.

"No! Wait!"

He paused, looking up at her. "Holly... Please. Please let me. Please let me taste you..."

He was dizzy with it, the scent, the taste, the sight, so close. He couldn't bear to think she might deny him. "Please..."

She looked at him for a long moment. He feared he knew what was going through her head. Presumably her ex-partner had been no better at this than anything else.

"Trust me, Holly," he whispered, and she hesitated then nodded, letting her legs fall open in a blatant gesture of trust.

Her faith in him almost brought tears to his eyes. What had he done to deserve such a gift? It was precious and wonderful. And now, he thought, he was going to give something back. He was going to give her the pleasure she deserved.

His body surged. Just the thought of tasting her was enough to make him lose it. Hanging on to his control by a thread, he lowered his head to her and, with a broad sweep of his tongue, caressed her softness.

Holly had read about this act, had imagined it countless times, had even written about it in one of her books. But she had never, ever thought it would feel like this.

As his warm, firm tongue slid over her, she cried out in shock, arching her body. The sensation was exquisite

He moved his tongue around everywhere—first lightly stroking her, then delving to press against her. She moaned and muttered. Something was building, a gathering storm.

Tension roiled within her. She tried to close her legs and Mac thrust them over his shoulders, preventing her from doing so.

The move seemed to give him even more access to her. He licked her from top to bottom and she cried out, keening.

A sheen of sweat dewed her body. She wanted him so much. She needed him... Helplessly, she fought to get closer to the delicious contact and he redoubled his efforts.

"Mac," she sobbed, not knowing what she was asking for, but it seemed he did, because in the next moment, he slid a long finger inside her.

She cried out at the blinding flash of sensation — gasped and arched. "Mac! Please, please..." A flood of pleasure ratcheted up her need. She moved, desperately trying to prolong the sensation, then suddenly he drew her clitoris into his mouth and sucked on it gently.

She exploded without warning, electricity arcing through her as she cried out and writhed as a whirlwind of sensations blasted through her. Beyond sanity, she felt him, still there with her, forcing the fire to burn until there was nothing left but sparks and embers.

Afterwards, she lay, shivering and shocked, sprawled out in helpless abandon. Mac moved back up the bed and took her in his strong arms. She smelled herself on him, just as she recognised the delicious, musky taste of him on her lips. They kissed, and he rested his forehead on hers.

"Holly…you are…a miracle. A force of nature. You are so wonderful…"

She wrapped her arms around him. "No. Mac. It's you. Unbelievable. I never imagined…"

She sighed as he gathered her up against him. His hardness pressed against her thigh. She reached down and stroked it wonderingly. He was as solid as a rock, and wet, too. He must be aching with need.

Drawing back, she asked questioningly, "Mac?"

He shook his head. "It's okay. It doesn't matter. Later."

But she didn't want to leave it till later. She wanted him to experience the explosive pleasure he'd just given her. And she wanted to see his face as he came.

Smiling slowly, she shook her head then encircled him with firm fingers. He looked at her, and he widened his eyes as he read the intent in hers.

"You don't have to," he said hoarsely.

"I want to."

Slowly, she slid down him and tentatively licked him. He tasted clean and faintly salty. He jerked, bucked and a low growl rumbled from his throat.

Smiling, she took him inside her mouth, sucking him gently even as she caressed his balls. He twisted beneath her ministrations, and she could feel the heat coming off him.

The movements of his hips were increasingly frantic. He was close.

But what was it he had said? *'I want my first time with you...to be in you.'*

Drawing back, she slid back up to face him and kissed him deeply. Holding his face in her hands, she looked into his eyes, whispering "I want you in me."

The breath punched out of him. "Yes! Oh, yes. Hell, yes. Please..."

He reached over to the bedside table, grabbed a condom and rolled it on, done before she could blink. She leaned over him, brushing his chest with her soft breasts, and kissed him. "Thank you," she murmured.

Sitting up, she straddled him. He looked at her reverently, his eyes brilliant blue and glittering, his pupils languorous and enlarged. And without warning, she slid down on him and cried out at the hot wonder of the sensation.

There was no way it could last long. They were both so aroused that it was impossible to hold back. Mac grabbed her hips, even as she slammed down on him and they were both gasping and writhing as the tension built. Disbelievingly, Holly realised she was going to come again. The thought had no sooner formed than the world splintered. Explosive pleasure poured through her and she cried out.

Chapter Two

She was gone when he woke up the next morning. He reached out for her, needing her in his arms, and she was missing. His eyes flew open. No glittery dress. No silver sandals. No sparkly little evening purse. The bathroom door ajar and the room beyond in darkness. He was alone.

He rolled over and reached for her pillow, pressing his face into it. It still smelled of her—roses and musk. He squeezed his eyes shut and tried to pretend it wasn't to hold the tears back.

He wished desperately that she were still with him.

His body could still feel the imprint of her touch, the sensual memory of her fingers stroking his stomach, his legs, her lips around him, her beautiful, gentle kiss. She had taken him to a place he'd never imagined—a place of such powerful, passionate pleasure that he damn near trembled to think of it. He'd never experienced anything like it.

And the way she'd opened to him and let him touch her. He swallowed hard. For all her apprehensiveness, she had trusted him, had given herself without reservation. He had never experienced lovemaking so honest and real. She was breathtaking.

But she could never be his.

In a way, he was relieved she'd gone, he told himself gruffly. He didn't like what he was feeling. Grief. Loss. Loneliness. He shouldn't be *feeling* anything. They'd agreed — one glorious stolen night of pleasure. And that was what they'd had. And it had been wonderful. More wonderful than he'd ever imagined lovemaking could be.

Not lovemaking, he corrected himself firmly. *Sex.*

He couldn't afford for it to be anything else. He wasn't about to get involved, not with anyone. Definitely not. Especially not someone like her, who seemed to have the unnerving ability to get to him. No one apart from Emily had ever been able to do that. And she had turned out to be a gold-plated, cheating, lying mercenary bitch who had betrayed him and ripped his heart out. There was no way he would ever risk getting that involved with a woman again.

Since Emily, who had been quite a few years ago now, his relationships with the opposite sex had been brief and largely physical. They had suited him well. He had neither the time nor inclination for anything more. And he didn't now, he told himself fiercely.

But Holly... The thought of not seeing, hearing or touching her filled him with anguish.

Holly...

It had just been one night. That was it. That was all there was *ever* going to be with her. She'd made it clear that she didn't want more — and neither did he. He just had to make himself accept it.

He jumped out of bed, ignoring the clamouring thoughts, the emotional wrench at relinquishing her scent on the pillow. *A shower*. He needed a shower. And he damn well needed to get a grip.

After a hot shower, he felt calmer. The sex had been so much more than good. Naturally, he was going to mourn its loss. But that was all it had been. *Just sex*. He towelled himself dry, smiling at the faint finger marks bruising the skin on his upper arms, remembering how she'd clutched at him as she'd neared orgasm, her tight grip and wide eyes showing the kind of astonishment that suggested she didn't feel that kind of sensation often, if ever.

He reacted sharply to the memory. He could still see the awed expression on her face in his mind's eye. He shuddered, wishing he could give her a lifetime of pleasure.

Stop it.

He blocked the thought ruthlessly, pulling on his clothes with sharp efficiency. *Enough wallowing*. He had a huge amount to do today. He needed to get going. He was supposed to be meeting with the owner of Liberty Security at ten.

His mobile rang as he was putting his shoes on. He picked it up, smiling as he saw his sister's name on the display.

"Hi, Leonie."

But his face changed as he heard his housekeeper's voice on the line. "Flora? What's wrong? Why are you using Leonie's mobile?"

He listened intently as the conversation continued. By the end of it he was sitting on the side of the bed, his face ashen and his expression grim.

"Right," he said finally. "I'll finish up my business here as quickly as I can. I have to talk to the security firm... I'll fly home by tonight at the latest." His voice broke. "Flora, look after her for me. Don't...leave her, not for a minute. Please..."

He paused for a minute, then nodded sharply. "Right. Okay. I'll get moving. Keep me updated."

Thanking his housekeeper, he disconnected the call and sat staring into space for a moment. He swallowed hard. His life was one long, ever-darkening nightmare. But for his sister it was even worse. For her, it was completely inescapable. What the hell was he going to do? How was he going to put all this right? Things couldn't continue like this.

He got up restlessly, walked to the window seat and looked out at the glorious gardens, serene in the sunlight. They'd looked magnificent last night while he was sitting with Holly. He hoped she was all right this morning, that she'd left feeling happy and fulfilled. At least he knew she had walked away from the encounter with a positive memory of lovemaking.

How he wished that they'd had longer, so he could have shared more with her. He had a feeling she didn't know much at all about the many pleasures of passion. But regret was pointless. He'd had what he'd had, and he should count himself lucky. Many men went through their whole lives without meeting a woman like her. He sighed. He would hold on to the memory and treasure it. A moment out of time. But now he was back in the real world, and the real world was hell.

He turned and picked up his bag. At some point soon, he would have to get in touch with the organisers of the ball to get contact details for Holly. They would probably need to discuss his winning bid. His heart lifted momentarily at the thought. At least he would be able to speak to her again, just once more.

In his mind's eye, he saw the pile of *Wayfarer* books on the coffee table at home. Leonie had been living in them recently. He smiled. She had always been an avid reader, and her long-held ambition had always been to be a writer. She had never believed she could do it, had always seen it as a career for others who were cleverer, more talented. But she *was* talented. He had read short stories she had written, and they were gripping. If only he could ignite that passion once again, give Leonie something to enjoy, to work towards, to live for…

An idea started to form. It was an idea fraught with pitfalls, but at least it was something. From his point of view, it was the worst idea ever. But it might work. And at this point, he was desperate enough to try anything.

* * * *

Meanwhile, Holly sat at home in her sunny kitchen with a steaming cup of coffee and wondered what the hell had come over her the previous night.

Well, she knew what had come over her, but—

Shaking her head wryly at her sometimes inconveniently juvenile sense of humour, she took a swallow of her coffee.

She still could not quite believe the way she had behaved with Mac. It was as if every inhibition she'd ever had had flown out of the window, as if his challenge for her to be real, open and honest had released her from her reservations and fears and set her free. Until that had happened, she hadn't realised how reserved she had been, how much of herself she had been holding back.

She'd done things, said things, *allowed* things that she'd never even considered before. And it had been amazing. *Intensely liberating. Wonderful.*

He had been wonderful. Her throat tightened at the thought of him. He had been so kind, so reassuring, so careful and considerate of her feelings and her body. She had never imagined a man could be like that. Even when he had been completely lost in passion, he had taken care of her. It had been amazing. She smiled.

Not only that, but he'd been the most liberating and liberated of lovers, completely accepting of the side she'd never imagined she had. No, 'accepting' was the wrong word. He'd absolutely revelled in it. She felt a sharp pang of regret that one night was all she could have with him. There were so many things she wished she could explore and do.

But there was no way she could risk more than one night, even if he wanted to, which he didn't. He was a magnetic, dynamic, influential man, rich as Croesus — a man she should be running a mile from. And she had. The minute she had opened her eyes, she had realised she needed to get out of there. The night had been too good. Too magical. Too alluring. It made her want to do it again and again and again...with him.

And that just couldn't happen. There was no way she could get involved with a man like him. He was too much of a danger to her emotional equilibrium. He made her feel more than just passion. She *liked* him. She was *drawn* to him. He *appealed* to her. And that was terrifying. She had never felt like that about anyone, ever. Had never wanted to. Hated the fact that she did. What was happening to her? Had she inherited her mother's dangerous weakness for charismatic alpha males?

Nausea swirled. She was *not* like her mother. *Absolutely not.* There was no way she would ever, ever allow herself to be dominated and controlled by any man.

She really should never have gone to bed with him, though she couldn't find it in her heart to regret the experience. He had shown her what true passion, true pleasure, should be like, and that was a gift to her.

A gift that in some way she wanted to share. She stared blindly out of the window at the sunlit garden, thinking about Drake. If he and Isabella got together, that was what he would be like — powerful, but caring. Isabella had had a rough time of it. She wouldn't easily let a man like Drake touch her. But if Isabella suffered a trauma of some sort...and Drake rescued her, perhaps her defences would be down, and Drake could... But then, what kind of man would Drake be if he took advantage of Isabella's vulnerability at such a time? But maybe if Isabella came on to him...

Her imagination drifted. Drake would be the perfect lover for Isabella...

She got up absently, dumping her coffee cup into the sink. Maybe Drake could do something to help Isabella trust him... Randomly, she went to fetch her post. She hadn't opened yesterday's yet, in the chaos of last-minute preparations for the ball. Maybe she should put Isabella in an environment where she was trapped with Drake, so she couldn't run. A ship, perhaps... She opened stuff without thinking. There was the usual random mix — a load of fan mail forwarded on from her publisher. She should think about employing an admin person to help cope with that. There was also a pretty beribboned invite to the launch of a fellow author's book — *nice* — and a letter from her dentist reminding her that her check-up was due. *Damn.*

She set that last one to one side. She would force herself to call later to book an appointment. A package caught her eye, a brown padded envelope with a typed label. She turned it over. No return address.

Something else from a fan, perhaps. She occasionally received small gifts. She reached for a pair of scissors and cut open the top. What if they were trying to escape from the West Indies...if Isabella had the slaves who had helped her escape accompanying her...

Something grey and furry slid out of the packet and she froze then dropped the envelope with a hoarse cry.

The stench was horrific.

A *rat*.

It was a rat. A bloody, maimed, maggoty, extremely dead rat.

She backed away, her mind refusing to accept what she was seeing, there on the polished marble counter in her pretty, sunny kitchen.

A rat. A rat. A *rat*.

The sickening stench swirled around her, even as the corpse, its innards exposed, crawled with insects.

She bolted for the bathroom and threw up, retching until there was nothing left. *There is a dead rat in my kitchen.*

Exhausted and bedraggled, she sat on the bathroom floor, trying to control her breathing. The doors to the house were locked. She was okay. She was safe.

Someone sent me a dead rat.

It was on the counter in her kitchen.

Someone sent me a dead rat.

Her head spun, and she realised she was hyperventilating. Heat washed over her skin. She was going to faint...

No, she damn well was not. Grabbing the sink, she hauled herself up and turned on the cold tap. She pushed a limp hand under the icy blast of water. It sprayed out and she felt the vapour on her face.

The cold brought her back to her senses. She leaned heavily on the porcelain and stared at herself in the mirror. She was ghost-white. Even her lips were pale. There was fear in her eyes...

And that was not happening. She stood up straight. No bloody stalker was going to reduce her to a cowering wreck.

Her mobile phone was in her pocket. She pulled it out, thanking her lucky stars she hadn't left it in the kitchen, and called the number she had for Jenna Scott, the policewoman who'd dealt with the stalking case.

Fortunately, she was on duty. Holly explained the situation briefly and was reassured and relieved in equal measure when Jenna said she would be there straight away.

"Holly, are all your doors and windows locked?" Jenna asked.

"Yes."

"Good. Stay out of the kitchen. I'll be ten minutes."

At twelve fifteen, after a quick call to the administrator of the charity to get Holly's contact details, Mac caught a taxi to Holly's house near Hampstead Heath. His appointment with the security firm had been successful, even if the conversation he'd had with them had seriously put him on edge. Having all the dangers a rich man and his family could face spelt out to him had not made for pleasant listening.

But plans had been reviewed, actions agreed on and he was now at least assured that everything possible had been put in place to mitigate those risks. He and his family were as safe and secure as he could make them.

And now he was going to see Holly. His spirits lifted. Damn it, he was looking forward to seeing her again, even though he knew he shouldn't be.

But the simmering feeling of anticipation would not be suppressed. Just the thought of seeing her, of being near her again, made him feel lighter, younger, more carefree than he'd felt for months. The feeling was so odd and unfamiliar that it made him realise how grimly dark his life had been recently.

He closed his eyes, his mind retreating, as it had done so many times that morning, to the exquisite pleasures of the night before.

"We're 'ere, mate. Looks like trouble, though..."

The taxi driver's voice jolted him from the light doze he'd fallen into.

"What?"

"We're 'ere. That'll be fifteen quid, ta."

Mac shook himself awake, fumbled in his wallet and pulled out a twenty. "Keep the change."

"Cheers, mate. Think there's some bother going on over there, mind you..."

Mac looked blearily out of the window and came abruptly awake. There were two police cars parked outside Holly's house. He was out of the taxi and running before he knew what he was doing.

Fighting down a sharp shard of fear and a nauseating sense of dread, he hammered at the door. After a moment, it opened. Holly stood there, looking astonished.

"Mac!"

"Holly!" He had her in his trembling arms before he had time to process the wisdom of his actions. He pressed her against him, buried his face in her soft hair, kissing it and breathing in her scent. She was alive. Unharmed. Safe. "Are you all right, sweetheart?"

She wrapped her arms around him and gave him a quick, reassuring squeeze before pulling away from him, confused. "Yes, of course I am. What's wrong?"

"The police cars—"

Her frown cleared. "Oh. Yes. Right. I...had a bit of trouble, but everything's fine now. I guess you must be here to discuss arrangements for Leonie?"

"Ah...yes."

"Well, you're welcome to come in. The police are just finishing up, and we'll be able to talk."

He nodded, wondering just what the hell 'a bit of trouble' meant as he stepped into her hallway.

The house was like Holly—pretty and elegant. Mac just had time to note a sweeping staircase, the rich polished oak of the bannister burnished by sunlight and breathe in the sweet fragrance from a large bowl of yellow roses on a side table before she ushered him into the sitting room.

A tall, wiry woman in jeans and a shirt was standing by the beautiful Victorian fireplace. In her mid-forties, she looked tough, strong and forbidding. She had an unmistakeable air of authority. He would have guessed a detective sergeant or above.

He tensed. Whatever was going on, he would lay money on the fact that it was more than 'a bit of trouble'.

He sensed that Holly was going to try to usher him past the woman and into the dining room beyond, and forestalled her by holding out his hand to introduce himself.

"Hello," he said, evenly. "I'm Mac Sinclair."

Eyes narrowing thoughtfully, she returned his handshake. "Detective Inspector Jenna Scott. Haven't I seen you before? Are you...*the* Mac Sinclair? *Sir* Mac Sinclair? The architect?"

She must have seen his face in the media. He smiled. "I am." He settled firmly down on a nearby armchair, ignoring the look of dismay that flickered over Holly's features. "But call me Mac, please. I'm a friend of Holly's—"

"Well, friend's a bit strong. We only met last night—"

He arched an eyebrow at Holly, a wicked look in his eyes, and watched a crimson blush sweep over her cheeks. Hell, she was gorgeous when she was flustered.

Jenna Scott glanced at Holly, made a noise that could have been a choked laugh and sat down in the chair opposite him. Holly glowered and reluctantly perched on the sofa. He could see she was too polite to force him to move, a fact for which he was profoundly grateful, since he had no intention of going anywhere until he understood exactly what was going on.

He smiled benignly. "We may have only met last night, Holly, yet I feel as if I've known you for years. So, this trouble…?"

Jenna frowned. "Yes. As I told Holly, sending something like a dead rat in the post is unpleasant but not normally an indicator of danger. But the one Holly's received has been eviscerated, deliberately killed in the most unpleasant way possible to be distressing to the recipient. Coupled with the note —" She shook her head. "I don't like it. This feels like someone who is angry and inclined to violence."

Mac froze, the smile congealing on his face. A solid block of ice coalesced in his stomach. Holly was in danger? Someone had sent her a *dead rat*? And a —

"What does the note say?" he asked, abruptly.

Out of the corner of his eye, he saw Holly make a quick movement as if to waylay Jenna from her course of action, but it was too late. Jenna handed over her phone and showed him a photograph.

He winced. There was a grotesque picture of what had once been a rat but was now a set of gruesomely mangled remains, with a typed note beside it.

You next…

He breathed deeply, feeling the pressure behind his eyes. This was a serious threat. He knew it. He looked up and met Jenna's eyes. She knew it, too. Finally, he met Holly's and saw fear, defiance, anger.

"Okay," he said, roughly, "what's the plan?"

Jenna paused then turned to address Holly directly. "Holly, we need to be careful with this. This was calculated to horrify and to frighten, but the note is an implied death threat. Whilst I don't want to scare you unnecessarily, I do think you need to take some precautions until we find out who's behind this."

Holly frowned. "What kind of precautions?"

"Is there anyone you could stay with? Preferably somewhere far away from here."

"I... I don't know. I'll need to think about it."

Jenna nodded. "Start thinking. You need to be out of here by tonight."

Chapter Three

They went to the pub.

It was obvious to Mac that Holly was seriously distressed by what had happened, though hiding it well, and that she was in no fit condition to make any major decisions until she had calmed down and taken time to reflect.

A quick glance at Jenna's face had told him that she thought the same.

So, when Jenna had said that she and the forensic officers would be another two hours in the kitchen, he had seized the opportunity and invited Holly out for lunch.

She'd agreed — not because she wanted to be in his company, he thought ruefully, but because she wanted to get away from the house and the horror of the dead rat.

He'd asked her for a recommendation for a place to eat, so here they were at the St. George and Dragon. It was a lovely Tudor-style pub restaurant on the edge of Hampstead Heath, white-walled and black-beamed with frothy hanging baskets filled with tumbling, sweetly scented scarlet geraniums. Beyond the dining room, there was a leafy outside area with wooden tables and a verdant lawn edged with budding pale pink roses that swept down to the slow-moving Thames beyond.

By unspoken agreement, they elected to sit outside at a small, secluded table not far from the water's edge. On such a beautiful sunny day, it was a pleasure to be out in the fresh air. Bees hummed as they drifted lazily from flower to flower, birds sang in the nearby oaks and a couple of ducks with a phalanx of tiny ducklings paddled past in tranquil contentment.

It was the perfect place to relax—calm, warm, comforting. The strain eased from Holly's features. The first genuine smile he'd seen from her that day crossed her face like a shaft of sunlight, brightening her countenance.

He smiled back. "Hi," he said softly, and the memory of the previous night's pleasures swirled between them. He looked at her mouth, the soft full curve of her lip, and his body quickened.

"Hi, yourself." She picked up a menu, but a faint blush on her cheeks showed that she was no more indifferent to him than he was to her.

He glanced down at the choices. "Any recommendations?" he asked.

"Hmm… They do a nice ploughman's…"

"Sounds good."

A pretty young waitress arrived and they gave their order, deciding on bitter shandies made with local ale to drink with the meal.

Mac grinned. "It's years since I've had a shandy," he confided. "My parents used to let me drink them as a teenager, because there's hardly any beer in them and lots of lemonade."

"Mmm. They're really refreshing on hot days." She crinkled her nose. "I don't really like drinking during the day, but I find a shandy quite refreshing."

He steered clear of any difficult topics as their meal was served, and they chatted lightly about books and films while they enjoyed their lunch. The cheese had been made by a local farmer and was deliciously creamy. The pickle was spicy and rich. The salad was crisp and fresh, and the bread was still warm from the oven.

Afterwards, Mac sat back, replete. "That was wonderful," he said.

"It was. And I feel much better now I've had chance to calm down a bit."

"Good." Out of the corner of his eye, he saw the waitress approaching to remove their plates. "Would you like dessert?" he asked.

She shook her head. "I'm done. But I would love an Earl Grey tea...with milk."

He laughed. "British through and through."

She grinned. "Guilty as charged."

He ordered her tea and a coffee for himself, and the peace of the afternoon seeped into them.

She glanced up at him, a smile in her eyes. "Mac, about last night..."

"Yes?"

"I... just wanted to say thank you. I had a wonderful time."

He felt something inside himself warm at her words. "Holly, you don't need to thank me. I should be down on my knees giving thanks for such an amazing woman —"

His breath caught as he had a sudden, vivid mental image of being down on his knees before her and how exactly he'd like to thank her.

From the hitch in her breathing, she'd shared the same vision. "I wish —" she burst out impulsively, then stopped.

"You wish what? The moon? The stars at your feet? Rainbows and unicorns? Just say the word —"

Laughing, she shook her head. "I wish… Don't you ever wish that you could just catch a perfect moment and hold it in your hand, keep it safe and treasure it? Stretch it out?"

He stared at her for a moment, his laughter fading into truth. He knew what she was thinking of. She was wishing their time out of time the previous night had lasted longer. He felt that too, desperately. He yearned with a deep, aching need for more of her.

He smiled faintly. "Had we but world enough, and time…" In another world, another time, maybe they could have been together. A world where she hadn't had an ex-lover who'd turned her off relationships and where he wasn't buried in responsibilities, obligations and dangers.

"You know Andrew Marvell?"

He looked up, sensing her astonishment at his knowledge of the metaphysical poet. "I do. I love poetry. And prose, too. I think, in another life, I would have done an English degree and developed my love of literature."

She looked at him curiously. "You didn't have the opportunity?"

He shook his head. "My parents died, and I had to take over the family business. It was just a building business then. I trained as an architect so I could develop it. It didn't leave any time for anything else."

"And now?"

"And now, there's just responsibility." He shrugged. "I don't regret it. My family have security, and I'm blessed with a good life in many ways."

"But you're not fulfilled? What you're doing doesn't enrich you?"

He stared down at the table. He'd never shared his feelings about his work. Generally, he was quite self-sufficient, not given to opening up or confiding in anyone. But with Holly, he felt like he could be honest in ways he had never been before. She made him acknowledge things he hid even from himself.

"Holly, I'd never admit it to another living soul, but no, it doesn't. Well, the designing part does, being creative, designing buildings that bring pleasure and sustenance to the soul through their beauty. But the business side of things...? No. I've always been good at it, but I don't particularly enjoy it."

"I see. I guess I'm similar in a way... I love the creative writing side of things, but the business element, managing the money, contracts..." She scrunched up her nose. "They make me want to run a mile. Luckily, these days I can employ people to do it for me – an agent, an accountant..."

He nodded. "Very wise. Play to your strengths. So, what about you, then? Did you do an English degree? Is that how you got into writing?"

There was a pause, then she said easily, "Nope. Just a good imagination, pen and paper."

"Really?"

"Uh-huh."

He watched as her gaze slid away from his. Something about this conversation was making her uncomfortable. He steered it back into what he hoped were easier waters.

"So," he said idly, "what moment would you stretch out if you could?"

"Oh!"

That beautiful blush was back. He couldn't help it. He laughed out loud.

Her eyebrows shot up. "What?"

"You're looking a little pink around the edges there, sweetheart."

"Ah." She rolled her eyes. "To tell you the truth, I'm not great at talking about this stuff."

"No, but you're bloody wonderful at doing it." The words slipped out before he had time to censor them. "Damn," he said with feeling, "I'm so sorry—"

But she shook her head. Mercifully, she looked shy but pleased. "I'm glad you think that."

"Of course I do. You were thinking about last night?"

"Yes. It was so wonderful... I wish it could have lasted oh...a couple of years, maybe. A decade. A century?"

A lifetime.

He suppressed the thought instantly. *No.*

Her hand was resting on the table. Without thinking, he reached out and laid his over it, then jolted with the awareness of skin against skin. He looked down at her delicate fingers lying beneath his—pink, pearly nail polish. Last night he'd caught a glimpse of it when she'd 'shh'd' him, just before she'd driven him right to the edge.

His body surged again. He should stop this. It was dangerous. It was stupid.

"So, if you could have stretched out the moment, what would you have done in it?" What the hell was he saying? He was a masochist. But he desperately wanted to know what she'd say.

Her flush deepened, then she squared her shoulders and looked into his eyes. And there she was, his vixen from the night before.

She gave him a sultry look that heated his blood. But then she grinned, and the impression changed. Now she was full of mischief, a woman who wanted to *play*.

"Well, let me see," she said thoughtfully. "If I had world enough and time... I would..." She paused and laughed self-consciously. "Oh, there are so many things I've never done but would like to try."

He squeezed her hand. "Name one."

"Oh. Well...I'd like to make... Ah, have sex... outside. Somewhere warm but private. I'm not an exhibitionist. A beach, with the sound of the sea..."

"Mmm." He nodded. "You'd do it in the sea or on the sand?"

"Oh! Err...both?"

"Sounds wonderful..." And it did. The thought of being intertwined with her on a warm sunlit beach, with the roar of the breakers and the scent of the sea and the cry of the seagulls in the background, made him ache. Or *in* the sea, with her long, long legs wrapped around his waist and the warm water lapping around her perfect breasts... *Hell...*

"What about you?" her quiet voice broke into his thoughts. "If you had world enough and time, what would you like to do?"

A thousand ideas tumbled through his head, each one more X-rated and indecent than the last. He gave a hoarse laugh. "Holly, if I told you, you'd run for the hills."

She smiled, shook her head slowly. "Truth, remember? I won't run. I promise."

He looked at her and she caught her breath, probably at his expression. His body was so hot, so hard, that it was impossible to disguise what he was feeling. A scalding flush crawled up his neck. "Sweetheart, I'd want to do everything. I'd bend you over the arm of that chair in your sitting room, lift up your dress and press myself into you. I'd kneel at your feet and kiss your ankles, your legs, the area at the top of your stockings, until you begged for more…or I did. I'd take tea and ice cubes to bed with us and see how you reacted to heat and cold…"

"*Tea?*"

"Mmm. Not scalding, but…hot. I'd take a mouthful and kiss your breasts…or maybe even other places… Would you like that, to feel the heat wash over you there? Would you squirm against my mouth? Moan for more? Then an ice cube straight afterwards…"

He swallowed, forcing back his arousal. Much more of this and he'd be disgracing himself. What the hell had got into him?

"Would *you*?"

"What?"

"Would you moan for more, if I did that to you?"

"If you—" A sudden, unbelievably erotic vision of her on her knees, taking him into her mouth, swirling hot tea or ice—or her tongue or any damn thing—around him made his heart seize.

He exhaled a ragged breath. "Yes," he said, unsurprised to find his voice coming out an octave deeper than usual, "I would moan and beg. Or more likely die of a heart attack on the spot." He shook his head. He had to pull back from this. "Sweetheart, I don't know if I'm going to survive you. You should come with a warning sign… Danger, too hot to handle!"

She laughed, blushing. He picked up her hand and kissed it.

She looked momentarily astonished. He closed his eyes. Dangerous was understating it. For this woman truly had no idea how exceptional, how utterly, impossibly sexy she was. And that lack of awareness made her even sexier. She was such a powerfully potent mix of naughty and naive...

He drew in a deep breath. "We should change the subject," he said, "before my body starts screaming for mercy."

It was already, but he wasn't about to tell her that.

She gave a sexy little wiggle that told him more than she knew about her own state of arousal. "Okay," she said, "what shall we talk about?"

A walk. He needed a walk...or something. What he didn't need was to be sitting here, talking to her like this anymore. There was too much temptation to tell her all the outrageous ideas in his mind. He'd barely skimmed the surface and that wouldn't do. He couldn't have this woman. One night, they'd agreed. He supressed a groan.

He was torturing himself.

"Fancy a stroll?" he said, abruptly.

She did. They finished their drinks, and he paid the bill, leaving a hefty tip, which made the young waitress serving them look as if her birthday had come early, then headed for the path that edged the Thames.

Tree-lined and tranquil, it followed the meandering course of the river. Across the water, in the distance, rows of Edwardian houses faded off to the horizon like an old watercolour painting, whilst beyond, the ghostly outlines of the Shard and the Gherkin shimmered hazy and pale against a duck-egg-blue sky.

Unable to resist, he took her hand as they walked along, quietly enjoying the view. The soft lapping of the water and the joyful sound of birdsong made him feel momentarily comforted.

But only momentarily. Now that Holly had regained some of her equilibrium, he knew he had the negotiating challenge of his life in his hands.

He reflected thoughtfully on what he knew of her. Successful. Independent. Sexy. But what had she said last night? *'I don't like being trapped...or pushed into things.'*

In the cold light of day, with what he now knew of her previous lover, that statement took on an unpleasant resonance. Her ex-partner had been rough with her in bed, he knew. Had he also pushed her into other things she didn't want to do? Maybe one of the reasons she didn't want to get involved with anyone was because she was afraid that they would try to control her, dominate her.

Although he wouldn't fancy anyone's chances if they tried it these days... The woman was a tiger, no doubt about it. Underneath the pretty, respectable exterior beat the heart of an altogether fiercer creature.

He really loved that about her, loved that she had let him see her secret self.

But that wasn't the point. He dragged his thoughts away from his technicolour memories of the night before and cautioned himself to think clearly. He needed to get this right. There was no way, no way in hell, he was going to let her run around London — or anywhere else — unprotected whilst some maniac threatened her. But if he said so, if she felt pushed around by him, he was sure that she would tell him where to go in no uncertain terms.

Moreover, he needed to persuade her to come with him for Leonie's sake. His gut clenched. He had to be home by tonight, with Holly at his side. How the hell was he going to do it? He sighed. There had to be a way.

Holly, who had been walking beside him wondering what on earth she was doing, glanced at him, curiously. She couldn't quite believe that having received a dead rat in the post, she had calmly come out for lunch with Mac and indulged in the kind of explicit sexual flirtatiousness she'd believed only belonged in red-hot romances. *Am I out of my mind?* She couldn't get involved with him. She couldn't. *No way.* She was already in too deep.

Because this wasn't just physical attraction. She really, really liked the guy.

Damn it.

But he looked as troubled as she felt, and she had a pang of concern. "Mac…is everything okay?"

A shadow crossed his face, and she knew with a sudden certainty that it wasn't. She stopped and pulled him round to face her.

Gone was the man who had flirted with her earlier. In his place was someone else — a man with darkness in his eyes.

Was he concerned about the same things she was? "Mac," she said gently, "we were talking hypothetically about what we'd do in another time, another world. You don't need to worry. You know I don't want a relationship and I know you don't. We were just…daydreaming, if you like. You've no need to look so worried."

His eyes widened. He looked considerably taken aback. Then he reached out and stroked a tender hand across her cheek.

"It's not that," he said, quietly. "I know you're not looking for involvement, that you only wanted one night. I know we were only…wishing."

"What is it, then?"

He rubbed the back of his neck. A muscle in his clenched jaw pulsed. She watched it throb, wondering what was making him so tense.

"I need to ask you a question. But you're not going to like it and I'm afraid of your answer."

Her mouth dropped open.

His gaze lowered. "I've been walking along trying to work out how to persuade you…how to re-negotiate with you, as if you were some damn business acquaintance. But you're not. You don't need my money, and you don't care about my power. I've got nothing to negotiate with. Nothing." He raised his eyes to hers and the raw vulnerability in their depths shook her.

He wrapped his arms around himself. She didn't think he was even aware of it. Something was hurting him badly.

He wheeled away from her to look out over the river at the ghostly outline of the city in the distance. His body was so tense that it almost vibrated with pain. She found she hated it…hated seeing him like this.

He stared bleakly out across the water. She took his hand and squeezed it. "Tell me, Mac," she said.

"Yes," he said, forcing the word out. "All right."

Silence. She looked out at the view, knowing he was trying to compose himself, sensing that he hated her seeing him like this. Weak. Exposed. She caught her breath. He was only displaying the same emotions that anyone else might feel, but she realised that he was such an alpha male that she had imagined him somehow immune to them, a caricature of a man rather than the real thing. Now she had to acknowledge that it wasn't so, that he was an ordinary person with feelings as well as power — someone who could be hurt.

It was a sobering thought.

In a voice rigid with strain, he said "I need to ask for your help with Leonie, my sister."

She didn't know what she had been expecting him to say, but it wasn't that. "Your sister?" she asked, cautiously. "How could I help her?"

"I told you my parents died when I was younger…"

"Yes."

"Leonie was thirteen when it happened. A car crash. I was nineteen. We didn't have any other family, so I became her guardian. Since then, I've tried to be father and brother…whatever she needed me to be."

Holly looked at him thoughtfully. Responsibility, he'd said, was what he had now in life — and the job he did provided his family with security. No wonder that was so important to him, given the difficulties of his early years. Nineteen was very young to take on parental responsibility for someone, especially a young girl on the cusp of womanhood, who must have been devastated at the loss of her parents. And not only that, but he'd also abandoned his dreams of studying literature to do so, had instead successfully taken over a business and qualified as an architect. It was a huge feat.

Holly grimaced, appreciating just how tough it must have been. "It must have been difficult, but she was lucky to have you. How old is she now?"

"Twenty-four."

She nodded. "You're still close?" She assumed they must be, for him to pay two million pounds to get her name into one of her books.

"We love each other."

There was something odd about that answer, as if he were evading the exact truth.

"Does she still live with you?"

"Yeah." He paused, as if gathering himself. "She didn't, until recently. She was at university here in London, doing a research degree. She was really happy. Really… But then…she… She was kidnapped."

"Oh, *no!*"

Shocked, she reached out and grabbed his hand. She couldn't bear to see him suffering so badly without the comfort of at least a touch.

He squeezed her fingers, held onto her grip as if it were a lifeline. "It took us three weeks to get her back. A lifetime. Eventually, we found her, and the kidnappers were apprehended. She came home to me…but she's a different girl. She won't go far from the house at all. I couldn't even get her to come to London with me for the ball. Then last night…" He stopped, squaring his shoulders. "Last night, whilst I was busy escaping and forgetting and enjoying myself, whilst I was dancing and…and…stealing *time*, she tried to kill herself."

"No. Oh, Mac…"

His shoulders slumped. "I knew I shouldn't have left her. I should never have risked it."

He looked at her, and the tortured expression in his eyes horrified her.

"Since the kidnapping happened, she's just buried herself in the *Wayfarer* books for hours on end. She's using them to escape, I think."

"Yes…"

"Then she saw a news item on the Internet about your auction. I thought, if I could win it for her, it might cheer her up a bit, so I came to London—only for one night. I just needed to get away. I let her down. She can't escape, but I tried to. I was wrong."

The guilt was plain in his voice and she couldn't bear it. She pulled him into her arms and held on tight. "Mac, no," she said. "You love your sister, but you can't make her decisions for her. If she tried to kill herself, even if anything had happened to her, it wouldn't have been your fault. She's a grown woman. She has the responsibility over her decision to live or die…not you."

He bowed his head. "I hear you."

But he didn't believe her, Holly realised. Responsibility, he'd said, but she had a feeling she'd only just skimmed the surface of what that meant for him. It was clear that he felt responsible for his sister's welfare, maybe even her life.

"Mac, what did you want to ask me?"

He looked up at her with a desperation he couldn't hide. "This morning, I woke up and you weren't there. I so wished you had been, but I understood. All we could do was offer each other a brief reprieve from reality. Then my housekeeper called and told me what Leonie had tried to do and I realised that everything I have, everything I am, is not enough to help in this situation, not enough to make her want to live. And I tried to think of something — anything — that might give her the will to survive. And there was only one thing I could think of. Only one thing in the world."

"What was it?"

He looked at her steadily and took a deep breath. "Holly…it was you."

Chapter Four

"Me!" Her voice came out as an embarrassingly high-pitched squeak. "What do I have to do with any of this?"

There was a long pause. Mac appeared to be thinking over what he'd just said.

Then he looked at her sombrely. "Not a damn thing, and I shouldn't be doing this. Shouldn't be putting this on you, dragging you into it. It's not fair." He slumped. "Forget I said anything, Holly. I just realised what I was asking you and it's too much." He turned to look at her. "I'm sorry. I shouldn't have told you any of this. You have enough trouble as it is."

Holly looked at him in exasperation. "Mac, I still don't understand what it is you *are* asking."

"It doesn't matter."

"Yes, it does. If there's something I can do to help your sister, I want to know what it is. You think I could turn my back on her? What kind of person do you think I am?"

"I—"

"Damn it, Mac, tell me!"

He took a deep breath then blurted it out. "Leonie... It has always been her ambition, ever since she was a little girl, to be a writer. She's always written stories, but she lacks the confidence to pursue writing as a career. You are her favourite author, the one she most admires by far...and I thought if I could get her into her writing again, give her some belief in herself, give her some ambition and hope, that it might just bring her back."

"You want me to encourage her to write?"

He gave her a sad smile. "Amazing what mad plans desperation can produce. Basically, yes. I thought we could say you'd come to meet her before putting her in your book, which would be true. But I hoped she might be persuaded to show you some of her stories...and you could encourage her. That might be enough. I know it's a long shot, but—"

"But it's the only shot you've got."

He was right. It was a long shot. But given the absence of any alternatives, it might be worth a try.

But then there was work, and the pressure of it was no small thing. The television series was in the can and the next one wasn't due to start until the autumn, but there was still the deadline for the next book to consider. "I know this sounds crass, but I've got writing deadlines..."

"That's no problem. You can work there."

She looked at him, seriously. "If I do this...nothing changes. I still can't..."

He reached out and pulled her into his arms. "I can't either," he said. "But friends... Perhaps we can be that. What do you think?"

71

She pressed against him and her heart rate quickened at the familiar musky scent and muscular feel of him. It would be difficult to be friends, to be around him and not give in to her desire. The man was a walking temptation. But it would be worse never to see him again. Besides, she only had a handful of friends, and none of them were male. This would be a whole new adventure. She smiled.

"Friends," she said huskily. "Your negotiating skills weren't so bad after all. You did have something to offer. It's a deal."

* * * *

He was like a force of nature, she thought later — unstoppable. No sooner had she agreed to go than he was arranging everything. Within five minutes it had been agreed that they should leave for his home at five, his team of cleaners had been tasked with scouring her kitchen and security had been engaged to keep an eye on her house and check any post for unexpected nasties.

That he had security on speed dial was disturbing. When she commented on it, he explained. "When Leonie was kidnapped, I employed a specialist firm, Liberty, to work with the police to find her. They're very exclusive, very private and very discreet. They do all types of security and personal protection work."

He looked away from her and clenched his jaw. "I became worried that the police were more focused on catching the kidnappers than on keeping Leonie safe, so I brought them in. The police weren't pleased at first. But...Liberty managed to find Leonie and steal her back. Then the police went in and arrested the kidnappers." He smiled faintly. "The police were happy. They got their culprits and all the glory for the arrests. Liberty was happy. They don't want publicity. They don't want any would-be kidnappers knowing of their existence."

"The security firm managed to find her?"

"Yes. Thank goodness. Anyway, the lead on the case, James, brought her home, and he's been staying with us on and off ever since. His presence seems to reassure Leonie, and he seems to understand what to say to help her. She won't speak to a psychiatrist or anyone else about what she went through, but occasionally, she tells James things."

"Not you?"

A look of pained regret flickered across his face. "No, not me. I think she's ashamed. She has nothing to be ashamed of, but James says it's normal for people who have been caught and trapped to feel like that."

Holly was profoundly glad he was looking at his phone as he spoke. She felt his words like a punch in the gut and a faint sweat sprang out on her brow. She hadn't thought of Leonie's experiences in those terms. She thrust her hands into her pockets to hide her clenched fists.

He glanced up, absently. "Anyway, I've learned from my mistakes. I've always taken some precautions. When you have money, I think you have to. But I'm working with Liberty to put things in place to make sure nothing like this can happen again."

"I see."

"Besides, having some security around seems to reassure Leonie. And on the plus side, it'll mean you're protected whilst Jenna goes after your creep."

"Ah...yes, I suppose it will."

"Right. I've sent a text to Jenna to let her know where you'll be. Shall we get a taxi back to yours for you to pick up your stuff?"

* * * *

At five o'clock they emerged from a taxi into a busy central London street. Before them was one of the most magnificent modern buildings Holly had ever seen. The spectacular glass-and-steel creation was stunning. It was shaped amazingly like a candy twist, and the sunlight glinted and sparkled off it in all directions.

"This is one of your buildings?"

He nodded. "Yes. This is my London hub. Most of my UK business is done here."

"It looks like a—" She broke off and flushed. It wasn't exactly polite to say that his design reminded her of confectionary.

"Like a what?" He grinned at her. "Go on. Be honest."

"Like a candy twist."

He nodded, pleased. "Do you like it?"

"Oh, yes!"

Looking gratified, he ushered her inside the sunlit lobby. "Does it remind you of your childhood?"

No. Thankfully.

She smiled. "It makes me think of light-hearted things. Even though it's very modern, it feels almost nostalgic."

"A candy twist was exactly what I wanted people to think of. I like a bit of whimsy in my buildings—something that makes people smile. At the same time, I like to create things that are beautiful, and I always think that curves and twists are. Most people are used to seeing buildings that are all straight lines, but they don't have to be. Buildings can be more sensuous than that."

"Yes..." He was right, now that she thought about it. When she reflected on some of her favourite buildings in the world – the Sydney Opera House, the Coliseum in Rome, the Burj Al Arab in Dubai – they were all curved, graceful constructions. She had never really mentioned architecture very much in her books, but perhaps she should put a spectacular place in her next story, have a building that became almost a character, influencing and shaping the lives of those who inhabited it.

They entered the building, walked across a vast sunlit atrium with its own tinkling fountain and entered a glass elevator which floated upwards in an impossibly smooth and silent manner. The view of London, with St. Paul's Cathedral, Big Ben and the London Eye, with the sparkling river Thames running through it was spectacular.

She glanced uneasily at Mac, so secure and relaxed in the grand surroundings. Here he looked the epitome of the successful businessman, on top of his game with one of the most powerful cities in the world at his feet. Here, his power was almost tangible. He had made, and owned, this vast edifice, built on one of the most expensive bits of real-estate in the country.

She could see now that he was more powerful even than –

She cut off the thought sharply – she would *not* think of the past.

But she shouldn't be here. The realisation was sudden, absolute and devastating. She shouldn't be anywhere near a man like Mac, a man who had more resources and power at his disposal than she could dream of. She knew what powerful men were like…

She should never have agreed to come. She'd allowed herself to be blinded by her physical attraction to him and by an appeal to her better nature to help his sister. She hadn't realised how much she was putting her trust in him until now. She swallowed hard, feeling the glass walls closing in on her.

Then the doors opened and she stepped out into the swirling wind and noise of a helicopter landing pad.

She was on the helicopter before she had time to work out what to do. Her hands shook as she fastened her belt, and Mac, who'd sat down beside her, cast her a quick, concerned glance.

He passed her a pair of headphones and put some on himself. "Holly," he said, "are you all right? I never thought to ask if you were afraid of flying."

She swallowed hard. It had all happened so quickly…too quickly. If she hadn't been so discombobulated over that damned rat, then distracted by her own physical response to the man…

She hadn't even let anyone know where she was going—not Melissa, not anyone. But Mac had told Jenna. *Mac* had told Jenna. She only had his word for it. What if he'd lied? Her stomach clenched, and she thought she might be sick.

At that moment, they rose into the air. Mac took her hand and squeezed it reassuringly, even as he called for a steward. A moment later, Holly found herself holding a glass of sparkling water with ice, lemon and mint.

She didn't even know where they were going. She was travelling with a man who could easily make the *Times* 100 Top Richest Men in the UK list, to an unknown destination. All she did know was that there would be security there...and a sister.

But what if the security was to keep people *in*, rather than keep them out?

No. She was being ridiculous. Mac was a perfectly decent man, an internationally renowned man who'd been *knighted*, for goodness' sake, and who'd done nothing, nothing at all, to make her think he was anything less than on the level.

Sweat beaded her brow. Memories that she was usually able to suppress hit her like hail – the tall, wired fences of the commune where she'd been born and raised, the guards, mocking and threatening, and the look of Anton Deveraux, the all-powerful cult leader and father figure, as he'd approached her, rabid desire in his eyes.

'*You're nearly thirteen...*' he'd said, softly. '*We'll marry on your birthday.*'

She'd been horrified and frightened, though not stupid enough to show it. She'd seen what he and his guards did to people who displeased him, though it didn't happen very often. Most of the cult members, including her mother, had followed his every word with a slavish devotion. Instead, she'd pretended to be honoured and excited as he ravaged her mouth with his sloppy lips and slimy tongue.

She had begun desperate plans for her escape that very night. And now she was back with another horribly powerful alpha male, trapped in a helicopter, going to who-knew-where. She retched. She was going to be sick...

A brown paper bag was thrust into her hand. She leaned forward, breathing deeply, trying to fight back the nausea. She was shaking from head to toe. She couldn't help it. Mac loomed over her, putting his hand on her back. She flinched away sharply and he quickly removed it. "We're nearly there, Holly. Another five minutes…"

"Where… Where are we going?"

"Oh! Not far. The Isles of Scilly."

Where the hell are they?

As if he'd read her thoughts, he said, "They're only about twenty-five miles from mainland England. It's a small archipelago, very pretty. The islands catch the edge of the Gulf Stream, so the climate is sub-tropical, and there are lots of spectacular tropical flowers and plants. The island we're going to is called St. Arthelais. It's lovely. I think you'll like it."

An island. She would be even more effectively trapped than she had been in the compound. But other people would live there. It wasn't like with Anton. People wouldn't be in thrall to Mac. She could always appeal to them for help if necessary. She took a cautious breath, trying to keep calm. She was over-reacting. There was no logical reason for her to feel threatened.

He continued to talk, and she knew he was trying to distract her. He was a nice man, a good man. She knew he was…if there was such a thing. Impatiently, she shook her head. Of course there was. He was. He *was*.

A few minutes later, the pilot announced they were landing, and they began to descend.

A short time later, they stood on the tarmac as the helicopter took off again. The landing pad was nothing more than a circle of concrete set into heather and gorse moorland. Beyond the drifts of purple and gold there were only sheer cliffs and the silver-shimmering sea.

Mac breathed in the salt-sea air and the green scent of ferns and heather, absorbing the soothing sounds of nature — the wind brushing through the grass, the cry of seagulls, the omnipresent low, thundering pulse of the ocean. And damn, he needed that soothing just now. He felt sick at the very thought of going home and facing Leonie, knowing he'd let her down, knowing he should never have left her.

As the helicopter departed, he took a bracing breath. This island was his favourite place on earth. Quiet and lovely with an almost tangible sense of peace, it always calmed him. He tried to draw it to him now, that sense of stillness and tranquillity, to ground himself against his anxieties.

He looked at Holly, again noting her pallor. Hopefully, now that she was out of the helicopter, she'd be all right. He'd been taken aback at her reaction to the flight. She'd not shown any signs of nervousness before they got on board. Maybe it was just delayed reaction from the events of the morning or lack of sleep from the night before. Still, the warm, clear island air should help her stomach settle.

It was a beautiful evening, with mellow golden sunshine and a light, refreshing breeze. A gentle, reviving walk might help her regain her equilibrium — and might help him find his, too. He really needed to, before he spoke to his sister. He absolutely did not want to talk to her until he was sure he wouldn't say anything to upset her even more.

"I…ah…took the liberty of asking the pilot to send a message to say we'd walk to the house. It's not far, and I thought perhaps the fresh air would make you feel a bit better. I can arrange for a ride, though, if you prefer."

But she shook her head. "Walking's fine."

They set off at a gentle pace, following a narrow gravel path up the incline of a small hill. Her head was bent as she concentrated on the uneven path, but he was concerned to see that she was still trembling.

"I hope you'll like it here," he said, easily. "This is my favourite place in the world."

"You're...uh...from here, originally?"

"No." He paused as a beautiful pastel-blue butterfly with white edging fluttered past. "That's an Adonis Blue," he said, quietly. "They're a rare breed. They need grasslands, and there aren't so many of those about these days. You see the little yellow flowers?"

She looked out at the scrub grass, purple heather and clumps of tiny golden blossoms stretching out towards the sea. It was exquisitely beautiful. "Mmm-hmm."

"It's horseshoe vetch. That's what they feed on." He smiled. "That's one of the reasons I like owning this island. I can make sure it remains unspoiled, a haven for wildlife."

"Yes, I — Wait. You *own* this island?"

She seemed to stumble for a moment, and he put his arm around her tense shoulders to steady her. He felt a faint tremor and wondered with concern if she still felt nauseated. "Yes. It's perfect for peace and privacy when the rat race of London and New York get too much."

"That's... That's where you normally live?"

He shrugged. "Mostly. It's where I own houses. I tend to travel a lot to wherever the work is."

"I see."

"So...how many people actually live here?"

He shrugged. "Oh, just us and our housekeeper Flora and her family. Her twin son and daughter are at university at the moment, but they come back during the holidays. A lot more people live on St. Mary's, which is ten minutes away to the southwest—maybe a thousand or so."

"So, there are only a handful of people living here?" she said faintly.

"Well…we often have visitors, but yes, usually." They were almost at the top of the hill. "In a minute, you'll have a great view of the islands."

They crested the top of the slope, and Holly gasped. He wasn't surprised. The view was one of the loveliest he'd ever seen—and he'd travelled extensively. From their vantage point, the whole of the island could be seen, tiny in comparison to the vast ocean surrounding it. On one side, pink and purple heather-covered moorland swept down to a natural bay and a small harbour, with a golden sliver of beach edged by turquoise and aquamarine sea. On the other lay some small fields, a cove with a beach and cliffs. Beyond lay the islands, mirage-like, ephemeral in a silver sea, and, more distantly, the Atlantic Ocean, stretching out to the far horizon.

"Oh!" Holly's stunned exclamation satisfied him. He was surprised at how much he'd wanted her to like it. He glanced down at her. In the soft light, with the breeze sweeping soft strands of hair across her face, she was breathtakingly lovely. His stomach knotted with a sharp surge of desire.

He turned abruptly to look out at the rolling sea, the breakers foaming against the cliffs, and wished for what seemed like the thousandth time that things could be different, that she could be his. But there was way too much trouble in his life for her to be part of it, even if she'd wanted to be. The problem was, she was too damn appealing by half. He needed to keep his distance.

He stared at the moss-covered granite at his feet. A tiny, delicate purple and lemon dwarf pansy flowered from between the rocks. He swallowed. It was a rare flower — precious and endangered. In the whole of the Britain, it grew only on the Scilly Isles. And he could have crushed it so easily. One careless step and it would be gone. His stomach twisted. Life was like that — so fragile, so vulnerable, so exposed.

His parents had been taken, wiped out by the careless swerve of a drunk driver in one horrific moment. Leonie could have died at the hands of her kidnappers… And Holly too could be hurt, killed by some maniac who was maybe just warming up by sending her dead animals.

Desperation rose inside him and he forced it down. He didn't know how to bear it, the weight of his fear. There seemed to be danger everywhere.

He shouldn't be worrying about Holly. He had enough on his plate worrying about Leonie. Holly was not his to be caring about. She was just an acquaintance. *A lover*, an insidious voice inside him whispered. *A one-time lover*, he corrected himself, savagely.

He hadn't felt so desolate since his parents had died. The sea and sky merged in endless blue to infinity. They would be there long after he and all his petty troubles were gone. But in the meantime, he needed to tread carefully, to shelter the precious flowers in his care.

He ran a rough hand through his hair, entirely unaware that Holly had been watching the expressions flicker across his face in painful clarity.

And for Holly, that watching had been a stunning revelation. As she'd stood at the top of the mount and seen just how utterly isolated they were, she'd experienced a sense of vulnerability that was unbearable to someone who had once escaped a situation of utter helplessness and sworn never to be put in that position again. She'd been ready to cut and run, to demand that he take her back to the mainland *right now*.

But then she'd seen his face. He'd looked at her, just for a fraction of a second, and she'd seen longing. Then he'd turned away from her, his body language speaking of defeat and despair. And his expression in profile? She swallowed. It was the look of a man with an unbearable emotional burden, not the look of one with too much power who was willing to use it against others.

She realised with a jolt that she had made him a monster in her mind. She'd focused only on the parts of him that she feared — his power, his wealth. She'd overlooked the part of him that was vulnerable — the man who needed help with his sister, who had responsibilities hand over fist but apparently no one to turn to for comfort.

She stepped forward and turned him to face her. He flinched at her touch on his arm but did as he was bid. His eyes remained firmly fixed to the ground and she was aware that his hands were balled into fists.

"Mac," she said softly, "look at me."

He raised his eyes to hers. What she saw there made her wince. That he was trying to hide his emotions was obvious. That he was failing, equally so. He was too upset, his distress too acute to conceal.

What was it that was hurting him like this? She thought for a moment, then she knew. "You're worried about seeing Leonie?"

A nerve throbbed in his cheek. *Partially.* "Yes."

She pressed a soft hand to his face. "She's your sister and she loves you. If any wrong has been done" — which she highly doubted — "she'll forgive you."

He closed his eyes. "I don't deserve forgiveness," he said, hoarsely. "I should have known not to leave her."

"I think you need to forgive yourself." She spoke the words on instinct, without conscious thought, but winced at their bluntness.

"Yes, well, it'll be a cold day in hell before that happens."

He thrust his hands into his pockets. She hated to see him like this. Stepping forward, she wrapped her arms around him. "Mac, I know we're just friends, but—"

"You're a kind woman, Holly," he said, then without any hesitation, he bent his head to kiss her.

It was a kiss borne of need, of desperation, of distress. It should have been harsh and rough and brutal, but it wasn't. Instead, Mac took her in his arms with unmistakeable reverence and kissed her with something akin to adoration.

As he lowered his head, Holly closed her eyes. He brushed his lips against hers, warm and tender. Her body quickened and she moved closer, pressing herself against him. The clean, fresh scent of cedar and the soft musk of his body made her shiver. The night before she had tasted him, had breathed that same scent as she came.

Her stomach knotted and desire swirled as she lost herself in the darkness of the kiss, the warmth, that strangely wonderful sense of two merged into one, belonging only with each other.

She stroked the back of his neck, the smooth softness of his hair, the warm, precious skin. She wanted him so much, wanted to comfort him and take away his pain...

A kiss is not enough. She had to stop. With an acute sense of loss, she stepped back.

Breathing deeply, she pulled herself together. With lust abating, she was able to think more clearly. That had been a mistake. She was glad she'd done it, for his sake, but kissing him was just too damn intense, too dangerous and too much of a temptation. She couldn't let herself get any more drawn to him. The level of desire she was experiencing felt uncomfortably close to need. And she knew where that could lead. Hadn't she seen it in her mother? Her mother had been hopelessly, helplessly dependent on Anton for her emotional happiness. Everything revolved around the subjugation of her needs and wants to his. A frown from him could cast her into a pit of despair for days. And the level of power that gave the man over her was terrifying.

Well, she might have some of her mother's genes, but she refused ever to allow herself to succumb to what her mother had called 'love'. No, she was an independent, emotionally liberated woman and no man, however attractive, was going to lure her into that kind of emotional oppression.

She would not let him touch her again.

He drew in a ragged breath and Holly saw raw need and unadulterated hunger in his eyes before he veiled them. He gave a choked laugh. "Sweetheart, I" — he shook his head as if speechless, then sighed — "I...really shouldn't have done that, but I needed it. Thank you."

"My pleasure. But we should make a deal."

Her words echoed those they'd spoken the previous night. Then they'd made a deal to share nothing but truth between them. The intimacy of that agreement swirled around them now. Holly could see in Mac's eyes that he was remembering their promise to each other — and everything that had come after it.

As she was.

Damn it, that was not helpful. She cleared her throat. "Yes. I came here on the understanding that we would just be friends. I know that's what we both want."

He nodded, reluctantly.

"So, I think we should make a deal not to touch. We're too…too…"

"Too combustible? Too vulnerable?"

She winced. As much as it pained her to admit it, he was exactly right. When they touched each other, they weakened their resolve. "Yes," she forced out.

A muscle worked in his jaw. His tension and indecision warred in his eyes.

Finally, he sighed. "Much as I don't want to admit it, you're right. The chemistry between us does seem to be off the charts. I just look at you and I want you."

His blunt honesty shocked her.

"Truth, remember? I'm sorry if that truth offends you, but it's the way it is. I'll make sure it doesn't affect you, though. I'll not touch you again. You have my word."

Heat wrapped around her at his promise. *'I just look at you and I want you.'* He had described exactly how she felt about him. And that was why he was so dangerous to her, why they so desperately needed the agreement. She knew it but, like him, she didn't like it.

She should have been pleased that he had acceded to her request without opposition, but contrarily, she was conscious of a sense of loss, of something precious being discarded. But that was how it had to be, she told herself firmly. She could not afford to give in to her emotions, to become a simpering shadow of herself, a clingy, needy, desperate creature like her mother. No, she needed to stay away from this man, her Achilles heel, and keep her heart intact.

She nodded sharply. "Right. Deal."

A seagull screamed overhead, and for a minute she thought it was the loneliest sound in the world.

Chapter Five

Mac's home was unbelievable. At first glance, from a distance, it was difficult to see there was a house there because it blended so seamlessly with the scenery. Curved glass walls that seemed to undulate and ripple reflected the sky, sea and surrounding greenery to such an extent that it seemed she was looking at something that shimmered, as if it hovered between reality and fantasy.

As they walked down the gravelly slope and drew closer, it became more substantial. What had at first just looked like a copse of trees came into focus as a resplendent garden with palm trees, brilliant orange birds of paradise, elegant pink foxgloves and swathes of blue and purple delphiniums. Their glowing colours were mirrored in the glass of the house, making the garden appear to stretch into infinity.

Holly came to an abrupt halt. She had never seen — or even imagined — that such a house could exist. It was the kind of house dreams were made of — stunning, imaginative, enchanting.

What sort of mind could conceive of a house like this one? She looked at the way the building melded into the environment. *Not a mind that wanted to dominate the natural world or show off power over it.* The building was not aggressive, did not impose itself onto the landscape. Instead, it worked harmoniously with it. There was an element of humility about it. It celebrated the beauty of its surroundings whilst understating its own attractions.

Was this who Mac really was? Someone who did not want to draw attention to his own power, his own achievements, but instead cared more about the impact of what he did on who and what was around him?

She thought about Mac's regard of the rare butterfly. He'd really cared about it. And he'd said he liked owning the island so that he could make it a haven. Was this another way that his protective nature showed itself? She swallowed hard. She really liked this aspect of his personality, even as she worried that protectiveness could turn into oppression if taken too far.

She glanced at Mac and was surprised to find him watching her with a faintly vulnerable expression. He cast her a boyish smile. "Like it?" he said.

"I love it," she said, truthfully. "It's the most beautiful house I've ever seen. I'm awed by your imagination. It's amazing."

He flushed, and Holly was seized by a sudden urge to wrap him in her arms, to kiss him, to show him just how she felt about what he had created. But she couldn't do it. They had a deal, at her instigation — and for very good reasons. She really, really needed to keep her distance from him. She fought back the urge and turned to walk down the slope towards the house.

He continued to talk as they walked. "Yes, I wanted this house to have a kind of magical quality. This island has always felt enchanted to me. It even has its own cairn—a burial mound. Legend has it that the island belonged to King Arthur and was once part of the lost kingdom of Lyonesse."

"Really?" Holly could imagine it. There was something preternaturally lovely about the island. It had that odd sense of still, quiet timelessness that ancient places sometimes did. A feeling that spirits long passed still lingered, that there was a benign presence hovering over it. It was a place that would make anyone want to lay down arms and just appreciate the sublime joy and beauty of life and the sheer pleasure of being alive. If she lived here, she'd never want to leave.

She said as much, and Mac cast her a questioning glance. "Not too isolated for you?"

"No. I like it."

"Some people struggle with it. It's a place that reads you, that forces you to look inside yourself. It makes you listen to your own thoughts—and that can be an uncomfortable thing if you're used to the noise and bustle of life drowning you out. It's not so easy to hide from yourself here."

She stepped carefully over a sand-dusted tree root, half-submerged under a thin layer of soil that crossed the path. "I'll take my chances," she said. "Being a writer does that to you, too. Forces you to look inwards—and you don't always like what you find. But I still love it."

"You find release in the creativity?"

"Yes."

"Me too."

They reached the bottom of the slope and headed for the house. Close up, she could see a low granite wall and a small wooden gate, which opened up into a flourishing cottage garden. Beyond, Holly caught a glimpse of a vegetable patch sheltered by a row of apple, pear and cherry trees.

Mac paused at the gate then straightened his shoulders, opened the gate and ushered her in.

A moment later, a pretty, young woman with long, tumbling brown hair hurtled out of the house and threw herself headlong into Mac's arms.

"Mac! Oh, Mac! Flora told me what she'd thought I did, but I didn't mean to —"

Leonie, Holly thought, as she watched the young girl cling to Mac like a drowning person to a lifebelt. She was small, slender, pretty, with — from what she could see — a similar bone structure to that of her brother's.

"Leonie, I—" Wrapping his arms around her, Mac buried his face in her hair and held on tight. "I... I'm just glad you're all right. I'm sorry I left you."

"What?"

Leonie became aware that there was someone else present. Looking over her brother's shoulder, she spied Holly. She stepped away from him, seeming flustered.

"Oh," she said, sheepishly, "I'm so sorry. I knew Mac was bringing someone home. I just forgot for a moment—" She broke off, a frown settling between her eyes. "Wait a minute! Don't I know you from somewhere? I-I—" A look of pure astonishment crossed her features. "Aren't you—?"

"Holly Mason, yes. Pleased to meet you."

Looking utterly poleaxed, Leonie glanced at her brother. "You brought Holly Mason *here*? But...how?"

Mac laughed. "I did. Let's go inside. I'll explain everything over dinner."

* * * *

An hour later, Holly was busy unpacking her clothes in the elegant bedroom she had been given. It was a beautiful room. Polished oak floors had been topped with a sumptuous rug in rich jewel colours. A huge bed with a billowing white duvet and mounds of soft cushions looked welcoming and comfortable. A large bowl of golden Asiatic lilies was set atop a side table, scenting the air with their rich perfume. But the real focal point of the room was the floor-to-ceiling windows, which provided a vast panoramic view of the billowing Atlantic Ocean, with the shimmering islands and tiny lighthouse in the distance.

Holly had gasped when she'd seen it, to the gratification of Mac's housekeeper, Flora. "Like it?" the older woman had asked with a smile.

"Oh, more than that. It's absolutely stunning!"

Holly looked out of the window again. In her mind's eye, she could see that view at night, with moonlight drawing a sparkling line across the water. And in the distance a schooner... Maybe Drake should be on board that vessel. Maybe it should not be Drake rescuing Isabella but the other way around. *What if something happens to Drake? What if he was kidnapped?* In her previous stories, Isabella had suffered much and Drake had always been the strong one, able to support her. But perhaps now she needed to turn it on its head. Maybe he could be kidnapped and have a terrible time in captivity...

An image formed in her head of the captor — a slave trader perhaps? The one who haunted the dreams of the freed slaves accompanying Isabella? They would have to face their fears to rescue Drake. And when Isabella got Drake back, he would be a changed man.

Not noticing her distraction, Flora asked her if she would like a tray of refreshments. Holly declined, shaking her head.

"I think I'll just unpack and have a shower," she said, easily.

Flora smiled. "Okay. Dinner's usually at eight, though everyone normally meets for drinks at about half past seven. Just come down when you're ready."

Holly nodded. "That sounds great. Thank you."

When the older lady had gone, Holly pulled out her mobile phone. She was almost sure now that Mac had no nefarious purpose in mind by bringing her here, but she couldn't help her concerns. Driven by the trapped feeling of being stuck on an island, she called Jenna, just to confirm that she had arrived. From her responses, it was clear that Mac had indeed phoned her and that she knew exactly where Holly was.

With a guilty sense of relief, Holly disconnected the call then realised she should also call Melissa. Now that she came to think of it, it was odd that Melissa hadn't called her to discuss the previous night's ball.

But that mystery was solved the moment Melissa answered the phone.

"Holly! Hi. I was going to call you, but to be honest, I only got up a couple of hours ago. I have the worst hangover in the universe. Simon ordered champagne and it went straight to my head. But what an amazing night last night. We made a fortune! Two million pounds on your lot alone! And oh, that guy, Mac Sinclair... I told you he was *hot*!"

Holly heard a muffled protest in the background and grinned. "Well," Melissa continued, tongue-in-cheek, "obviously, not as hot as some other people I could mention" — a snort — "but if I was single, if I were *you*, I wouldn't say 'no'!"

Holly laughed. "True. He did have a certain something about him."

Melissa squealed. "I knew it! I told you...midsummer magic! The rose petals worked!"

"Mmm. Well, to a degree. He might be a gorgeous guy, but I'm not about to fall in love with him...or anyone else, for that matter!"

Melissa chuckled. "If you say so, Holly," she said. "But remember, only yesterday you said you weren't interested at all. Just look what twenty-four hours have accomplished. You're admitting he 'has something about him'!"

Holly shifted uncomfortably. Melissa was right about that. She had let her guard down and now look where she was. *In the guy's home, for goodness' sake!* Though, mercifully, Melissa didn't know that.

But she wasn't going to be like her mother. She just wasn't. No way was she going to let herself fall for him. She wasn't that weak.

"I wasn't impressed with that compere, though," Melissa went on, blithely unaware of Holly's reaction to her words. "Very sexist. I've e-mailed to complain about him."

"Have you?" What with one thing and another, she'd forgotten all about him. "That's great. I thought he was out of order, too. Anyway, I was just ringing to let you know I'm away for a few days on a last-minute research trip."

"Oh, right. Where are you?"

It occurred belatedly to Holly that she shouldn't say where she was. It was unlikely that Melissa would tell anyone, but she couldn't discount the possibility. If she told Melissa about the rat, she surely wouldn't, but Holly didn't want to worry her. Hopefully, the police would find out who'd sent it and she would never need to tell her. So, she said vaguely, "I'm travelling around, so if you don't hear from me for a while, I'm fine."

"Oh. Okay—"

There was a muffled commotion in the background. Holly could hear Topsy and Tim, Melissa's two young golden Labradors, barking. "Sorry, Holly. Someone's at the door."

Holly laughed. "No problem… Catch up soon. Bye!"

She disconnected, smiling to herself. Melissa was her closest friend, and it would be good to meet with her soon to discuss the ball. But whether she'd tell her about Mac, she didn't know. *On balance, probably not.* After all, that night had been a one-off, and she didn't want Melissa to get her hopes up, thinking that there might be a romance in the offing. After all, Melissa had been encouraging her to get back into the dating game for quite a while now. As far as she was concerned, a five-year hiatus after a bad relationship was quite enough.

Although Melissa didn't know that her lack of enthusiasm for another relationship wasn't because of Taylor. She didn't know about the compound, or her mother, or Holly's fear that if she fell in love, she would lose everything—her sense of self, her freedom, her independence. No, Melissa wanted her to have what she had — a good and loving man who would bring her companionship and pleasure.

But that wasn't on the cards for her.

She kicked off her shoes and lay back on the soft bed. It had been a long day, what with one thing and another. She could see how she'd overreacted to being brought to an island and felt more settled now that she knew Jenna knew her location. But she still didn't like feeling that she was trapped here and dependent on Mac's goodwill to get off and back home. She would just have to trust that he was a decent man who would do the right thing if it came to it.

She flung an arm over her tired eyes. Trust didn't come easy to her, but she'd managed it last night and her instincts about him had been spot on. She'd trusted him to look after her body and he hadn't let her down. Indeed, he'd taught her things about it and what it was capable of that she'd never even imagined. His patience, his care and his attentiveness had ensured she'd not just been safe but positively cherished.

So now it was her turn to look after him. Maybe not in the same way, physically — they were definitely each other's kryptonite — but she could at least try to show her appreciation and affection for him by helping his sister.

She needed to steer clear of him, though. Part of her didn't want to. He was so tempting. But she was only there to help Leonie. She would be an idiot to allow herself to be caught up in his spell once more. Just that one single kiss up on the hill had shown her how easy it would be to be swept away on a tide of passion. She could still feel the imprint of his lips on hers and the latent heat simmering deep inside. It would only take a spark for it to ignite. And whilst the physical part of her wished it would, wished for the relief and satiation of that fire, in her heart of hearts she knew that it would be the worst idea possible.

She had an awful feeling that if she succumbed to her own needs and allowed herself to experience pleasure in his arms once more, she would not be able to separate the physical from the psychological, and she would fall for him. That would make her vulnerable and weak — and that just couldn't happen. She had risked her life to gain her freedom and there was no way she was going to lose her psychological liberty just because her damn hormones were playing up.

Deliberately turning her back on such deeply uncomfortable thoughts, she focused again on Leonie, who was, after all, the reason for her visit. From what the younger woman had said when she'd come out to greet her brother, Holly wondered if she had, in fact, tried to take her own life or whether someone had misinterpreted what was going on. If it were the latter, it would be a big relief for Mac. It might at least alleviate some of the guilt and the blame he took upon himself for failing to prevent her abduction and for leaving her afterwards.

Would Isabella feel guilty if Drake were taken? No, she didn't think so. After all, unlike Mac, Isabella bore no responsibility for Drake. But maybe Drake would feel guilty for being taken. After all, he was a powerful man, used to defending himself — and others, of course. In that respect, he was a lot like Mac. But if Drake blamed himself for being kidnapped, perhaps he would also blame himself for all the indignities and troubles that would befall him because of it. And that would shame him...

Thoughtfully, Holly got up and retrieved her laptop from her suitcase. Maybe she would just do some research on the psychological effects of kidnapping on the victim. Perhaps it would be sensible to do that anyway, just to make sure she didn't inadvertently upset Leonie by saying or doing the wrong thing — not that she planned in any way to allude to the younger woman's terrible experience. If she wanted to talk about it, she would. No, her plan was just to talk to her about her possible role in the book, and from there see if she could spin it out into talking about writing in general.

But perhaps it would be insensitive of her to include Leonie's name in a book which featured a kidnapping. Perhaps something different, but equally awful, should occur to test Drake and bring him and Isabella closer together. Maybe he should just be imprisoned somewhere…

She logged in and started to read.

When she glanced at her watch again, it was seven o'clock. Her research had triggered all kinds of ideas. She was now sure that she wanted Drake to be the victim, and Isabella, in one way or another, was going to have to rescue him then save him psychologically — and perhaps even physically as well.

A warm certainty ran through her. She could feel the plot forming, coming together, and her instincts told her it was going to be a good one…the best yet. But she needed to give it time now — time to let her subconscious do its thing. She knew from experience that more ideas would occur to her at random moments and the small notebook she always carried with her would soon be full of scribbles of half-formed ideas and thoughts which would later be woven into the fabric of the book.

Jumping off the bed with enthusiasm, she went for a shower before putting on her favourite dark green dress. Beautifully cut and made of some miraculous material that never creased, it was always the first item of clothing she packed when travelling. Glancing into the mirror, she nodded in satisfaction. She would do.

At seven-thirty exactly, she ran lightly down the stairs to seek out company and drinks. Once in the elegant hallway, she looked around. One door was ajar, and she spied Mac standing by an elegant-looking fireplace, nursing a brandy. Unaware of her regard, he stood with a bowed head, looking brooding and sombre and dangerously handsome.

I want to be in his arms.

Her pulse quickened. *No.* She would not allow herself to feel like this.

I want to kiss away that darkness.

No.

To her dismay, he was alone. Obviously, Leonie hadn't come down yet. If she wanted to keep her distance, it would be easier if there were other people around.

He hadn't seen her yet, and she considered turning tail and retreating, but at that very second, he looked up and saw her. His brooding eyes warmed with instant pleasure. But then she saw the moment he processed the fact that she was loitering reluctantly outside, and something in his gaze hardened defensively. A mask dropped into place, and when he looked up again, his expression was distant, polite.

Very distant.

She hated it. She wanted to rush over and hold him and bring back the warmth she'd first seen in his expression, but she couldn't. She was not going to be like her mother, trying to soothe and pander to a man's emotions, constantly striving to put things right in his world. Besides, she needed to keep apart from him. They'd agreed. And if her reluctance caused him to keep his distance from her…good.

With a subtle inclination of his head, he beckoned her in.

As she stepped into the room, she drew to an abrupt halt, because the living room had a tremendous, overwhelming visual impact. Her startled gaze was immediately drawn to a wall of panoramic windows framing a splendid sunset. Orange, gold and magenta streaks lit up a vast sky and reflected off the sea in a blaze of fiery beauty.

"Wow," she breathed, momentarily distracted from the tension between them. "What an amazing view!"

"Mmm." Mac's dark eyes ran over her slender form in its elegant dark green dress. "Yes. Wow indeed," he said huskily, and she found herself blushing, knowing he was talking not about the spectacular view but about her. She folded her arms.

He caught himself and flushed, coughed. "Sorry. Ah…drink?"

He looked down at his own as if he'd forgotten it was in his hand and set it on a side table. Holly narrowed her eyes as she wondered why he was so distracted. Something was on his mind besides her. "Yes, please," she said.

"Something sweet? Like last night?" he asked. He rolled his eyes as he turned away, as if exasperated with himself. "We don't have mead, but we have some sweet liqueurs—Amaretto...or Baileys, if you like something creamy."

He suppressed a wince at the seemingly unintended innuendo. Unable to help herself, she laughed. He glanced at her quizzically and his shoulders slumped. The tension between them gave. "Ah, Holly, I'm sorry," he said, ruefully. "I'm not thinking straight."

"Baileys would be fine."

"Coming up."

He poured her a glass and handed it to her.

"Thank you," she said appreciatively, then looked at him forthrightly. "So, what's wrong?" she asked.

He grimaced. "It's that obvious?"

Holly shrugged. "I'm a writer. I watch people. I notice details."

"Ah." He looked, she thought, as if he were wishing she wasn't quite so observant. He raked a hand through his hair. The resultant tangle made him look even more rough and piratical than usual. *Drake.*

Clearing his throat, he explained. "Leonie said that Flora was mistaken about her trying to... Trying to..." He took a swift gulp of his drink. "She said she went out for a walk by the cliffs. She was just stood near the edge, looking down at the waves hitting the rocks, but she didn't intend to jump. She says she's thought of it now and again, but she wouldn't actually do it."

The pain in his eyes at that admission was unbearable to see. Holly desperately wanted to reach out to touch him, to comfort him. *No.*

So she contented herself with a sympathetic nod. He went on. "Apparently, Flora was gardening when she saw Leonie in the distance, very close to the cliff edge. She panicked because she thought Leonie was going to throw herself off. I think the whole episode has unnerved the pair of them."

Holly nodded. "It must have been terrifying for Flora," she said, thinking of the older woman's kindly features. She had no doubt at all that if anything had happened to Leonie, Flora would have never forgiven herself.

"Yes. She's shaken up, all right. I tried to get her to take a week off, but she won't. She's always been protective of us. She worked for my parents, and when they died, she stepped in and looked after both of us. She used to take care of Leonie after school or if I had to go anywhere. She's like a mother to her."

"The kidnapping must have hit her hard."

Mac nodded. "It did. She was distraught. I've got her and her husband Pete — he does the garden and looks after the boat and house maintenance — both going to counselling now about it. They need help to cope with what happened — and the ongoing after-effects."

Holly nodded then said gently, "And you? Are you seeing a counsellor? What about the impact on *you*?"

For a moment he looked startled. It was obvious to Holly that he hadn't even considered himself. Then he shook his head. "I get by," he said.

Holly looked down at her glass, not wanting him to see how concerned she was. It was as she'd thought. He was the kind of man who worried about everyone else but didn't take a minute to care for his own wellbeing. Still, she had planted the idea of counselling in his head. It was up to him to follow through on it if he wanted to.

After all, trauma wasn't easy to get over, as she should know. Though actually, she'd never spoken to a counsellor or anyone else about her own experiences either. She winced inwardly. Even the thought of telling someone about what had happened filled her with shame. She couldn't bear the idea of being so exposed and vulnerable to someone else. She hadn't even told Melissa. But surely the strength and secrecy of those feelings indicated that they still had a great deal of power over her. Her reaction on the helicopter on the way here had indicated all too clearly that her feelings were still so raw that they had the power to obliterate logical thought and throw her into an emotional tailspin.

She should think about getting some help. She did need to get on top of her past. And she would. But…not yet. Soon.

But she was being a hypocrite, encouraging Mac to consider talking to someone when she hadn't herself, until now…

Keen to distract herself from her uncomfortable thoughts, she asked, "And Leonie… She's still refusing professional help?"

Mac sighed. "Yes. She just doesn't want to talk about it at all…only a bit to James. I phoned him this morning. He had to go back to London for a couple of days, so he wasn't here when it all happened, but he's coming tonight to stay for a week. I heard the helicopter about half an hour ago, so you'll probably meet him at dinner. When he's here, he seems to somehow…ground Leonie."

Holly took a sip of her drink. It was rich, sweet and lovely. She thought about what Mac had said — *'She didn't intend to jump but she's thought of it now and again'* — and wondered if the rational and the emotional were at war in the younger girl. When she had first escaped from the compound, finding herself alone, penniless and traumatised in a strange world, she'd felt like that. Her flesh had crawled with revulsion at having been touched by Anton and she'd wanted not so much to kill herself as to find relief from existing in her own repulsive body. Sometimes, even now, she felt like that. But her rational self felt guilty at not appreciating her hard-won freedom. Knowing how precious it was, she had felt intensely obligated to make the most of it, to do something productive with her life.

The rational side had won out, just, but it had been a close-run thing for the first couple of years as she had fought to survive in the worst of circumstances. She had often wished not for death but for oblivion. Maybe it was like that for Leonie, too. Maybe she wanted to escape the memories. Maybe she even felt guilty at not appreciating the freedom she had gained.

Her painful reveries jerked to a halt as Mac put two fingers under her chin and raised her face to his. Her breath stopped at his touch and she took a hasty step back. His hand dropped to his side.

"Holly." His eyes were dark and serious. "Where did you go? I lost you… And you looked like you'd gone to Hell."

Damn. She needed to be more careful about guarding her facial expressions. Because if she was observant, Mac was eagle-eyed.

She winced. "I… I was just imagining what it must have been like for Leonie," she said, hedging.

He shook his head, slowly. "No. It was more than that."

She glared up at him, belatedly aware of what her expression might have revealed. Her stomach knotted. She'd really messed up now. Because if Mac thought there was something wrong that he didn't know about, she highly doubted he'd let it go. His protective nature was too strong for that. And she didn't think she could lie convincingly enough to put him off the scent. "Fine," she bit out. "I don't want to talk about it."

He didn't like it. She could see that. A muscle jerked in his jaw. His eyes blazed, intent and piercing.

"Holly, if you're in trouble, you need to tell me about it."

"I'm not in trouble."

"You looked more upset just then than you did when you found the dead rat. What is it? You looked...scared."

Her temper flared. "I'm not scared—not of anyone or anything."

He looked at her. "Sweetheart, everyone's scared of something," he said, quietly. "It's natural. We're only human. And you will tell me. Now or later, you'll tell me."

"You'll be waiting 'til Hell freezes before I tell you anything!"

Storm clouds rolled across his face. "If that's how long it takes." His face was grim. "But you're hiding something, and whatever it is, it's bad." He paused then set his glass down. "You know you can trust me. You know I'll help. Whatever it is, I'm on your side."

"You need to back off," she said. "My concerns are my own and no business of yours."

"Of course they're my concern! You and I made love last night—"

She stared at him, all her fears flooding to the fore. This was the real Mac—one who was trying to claim rights over her, to own her, to force her to do what he wanted because *he* thought it was best...like Anton.

She felt sick. "No, we didn't. We had sex. And that doesn't give you any rights over me at all. So don't think you can start trying to push me around."

He took an abrupt step back, as if she'd accused him of physically pushing her.

"I'm not—"

"You are." Driven past the point of discretion, she told him straight. "You have an overdeveloped sense of responsibility. You think you have to protect everyone. But I'm an adult. I make my own decisions, take responsibility for my own actions and share what I want at my own discretion. Nobody bullies me into doing anything. I won't allow it. You have no right to push like this and I won't have it. So, you need to decide. You either respect me, my judgement and my wishes or I leave. *Now*."

He looked at her, his face utterly expressionless. He clenched his hands then slowly relaxed them. He breathed deeply. "You're right," he said, quietly. "I apologise."

But he's watching me like a hunter watches prey, she thought uneasily. She didn't trust his volte-face one inch. She tightened her fingers around her glass. "I—"

At that moment, there was a discreet cough. She swung round. Leonie was stood in the doorway, dressed in a loose dark-blue shift dress that draped around her in voluminous folds. Her eyes were wide. "Hi," she said uncertainly. Behind her, a young man appeared. She hesitated. "Umm...have we come at a bad time?"

Chapter Six

"No, not at all," Mac said.

Oh hell. Had they heard her announcing bluntly, *'We had sex'*? It was bad enough that she was having a full-on argument with her host on her first night in his home.

Wishing the ground would open and swallow her, she pasted on a smile as Leonie and the man—James, presumably—entered the room. Introductions were made, hands shaken and Mac, completely unembarrassed, promptly poured drinks for everyone.

Urbane and sociable, he engaged them all in amusing conversation as they waited for dinner to be served. One would never have guessed from his demeanour that they had just argued.

Until she happened to accidentally catch his eye. There was a moment of tension, a fleeting glimpse of pain and tightly held control, then the impression was gone and his face smoothed over into a mask of pleasant blandness.

Unnerved and distressed at the hurt she'd inflicted, Holly turned her attention to James. He seemed a very unassuming chap—slim, brown haired, softly spoken and mild-mannered. No one would ever notice him if they walked past him in the street. But there was something about him, some alertness or spark of sharp intelligence in his expression that made her think of a hunter. He wore his ordinariness like a disguise. She was sure of it.

And when she saw him that way, it was easy to imagine the kind of man beneath—one who could outwit kidnappers and who would surely be at risk of death himself if they ever discovered his intervention. It was a good job he was on the side of the angels.

Isabella might need a man like that, if she had to find Drake after he'd been kidnapped. Someone to guide her through the maze of negotiations and advise her on ways to outwit his captors.

At that moment, Flora came in to announce that dinner was served, and they all followed her into the dining room. With a view every bit as spectacular as that in the living room, the space was illuminated by the glow of the sunset and the flicker of candles on the table.

It was beautiful. As Holly sat down, she knew she'd never eaten anywhere so lovely. And she'd been to quite a few places in the years since she'd escaped the cult.

The meal was wonderful—chicken in a white wine and cream sauce with crisp roast potatoes and baby vegetables. Conversation flowed easily. Leonie was bubbling over with enthusiasm and questions about the *Wayfarer* books, whilst James chipped in with the occasional comment. It was quickly apparent that everyone present was aware of the stories. Leonie knew the books so well that she could quote from them. Mac had also read and enjoyed them, and they had all watched the television series. Soon the conversation was revolving around how successful the television adaptation had been.

"Oh, I love Matthew Jordan," Leonie exclaimed, rolling her eyes. "He's exactly how I imagined Drake would be!"

Holly laughed. He actually wasn't anything like she had imagined Drake. In fact, she had been highly doubtful when the casting director had suggested him. But the screen test had been something else. Before her eyes, the young twenty-first-century actor had transformed himself into an eighteenth-century renegade. It had been an utterly convincing performance, and she had been persuaded.

As it turned out, so were the fans who had drooled over his good looks, his wicked expressions and his 'tough man with a hint of vulnerability' persona. Isabella had been a hit too. Patricia Anderson, who played her, had been a virtual unknown before the show, but had made the role hers. She had been nominated for a Golden Globe in the US and a Bafta in Britain. In Holly's view, she richly deserved to win both.

The conversation segued easily into a discussion of how Leonie might be represented in the next book.

"I still can't believe you won that auction," Leonie exclaimed, looking at her brother with appreciation. But then her gaze dropped, and, for a moment, Holly thought she noticed a fleeting look of discomfort. "I saw in the papers that there was a lot of excitement about it. It must have cost you a fortune!"

Mac shrugged. "It was worth it. It was for a good cause. Holly is a patron of the charity…"

"Really?" James leaned forward and smiled at Holly. "Help the Homeless, wasn't it? What got you involved with that, Holly?"

It was a good question, and one that she didn't want to answer. How could she tell these people that she had once been homeless herself, and if it weren't for the charity, she would likely have been dead in a gutter by now?

She couldn't. Pasting on a polite smile, she said, "It's a good cause. It helps a lot of people, young and old. I don't believe, in this day and age, that there should be anyone forced to be without a roof over their head."

James nodded, though Holly did not like the thoughtful, perceptive gleam in his eyes. It felt as if he could see right through her to the secrets she held inside. But then he smiled, and he was once again mild-mannered James.

As Leonie went on to ask Holly about how she came up with ideas for her books, Mac tuned out. His mind was too full of their previous conversation for him to attend fully to what was being discussed.

Had Holly been right? Did he have an—how had she put it?—'overdeveloped sense of responsibility'?

As the conversation flowed, he thought about what she'd said. His initial, wounded, defensive knee-jerk reaction was to disregard her words, to dismiss them as the opinion of someone who didn't understand.

But the trouble was, he had a sinking feeling she understood all too well how he felt. She was an unnervingly perceptive woman, and she'd recognised in him that compulsion to protect and shield those he loved. She probably saw where that compulsion had originated—in the loss of his parents. When they'd died, things had quickly spiralled out of control and he'd been fighting on all fronts to stop the ship from capsizing, struggling to keep the business afloat, even as he'd tried to cope with Emily's betrayal and his and Leonie's grief.

Had that struggle been so difficult, so traumatic, that he now couldn't relax and let people step up to take their own responsibilities in life?

Was this what Holly had been trying to tell him by the riverbank in London? That it was Leonie's choice to live or die and that he really was not responsible for it? That his responsibility was to love, support and protect her as best he could, but beyond that, her decisions were her own?

Naturally, having raised Leonie as a teenager, he felt responsible for her. He guessed most parents felt like that about their children. But his parents had gradually loosened the strings of parental guidance as he'd got older. By the time he'd reached nineteen, he'd been standing on his own two feet, and they had positioned themselves as sources of advice—but only if he asked them for it. They'd given him his independence and autonomy as an adult to make his own calls, his own mistakes and he'd learned from them to become a capable, confident man.

But he could see he hadn't done that with Leonie. Oh, he'd let her make her own decisions—to a point—but then he'd taken over. When she'd said she wanted to study in London he'd agreed, but then he'd set about finding suitable accommodation that was safe and pleasant for her, rather than letting her sort things out for herself.

And he'd instructed her as well about precautions against kidnapping — even before the abduction had happened, he had been theoretically aware of the risks — warning her never to drive with the roof of her convertible down in the city, to stay alert, not to walk around on the street with earphones in...

He'd instructed her, rather than giving her the information so she could make informed decisions for herself. And what had happened? She'd behaved just as a teenager would when issued with edicts from a parent. She'd instantly gone against them. She'd been taken from her car whilst turning in to a side street when coming home from a day at the beach. She'd had the roof down, the music on and she hadn't noticed what was happening until it was too late to do anything about it.

Not that he thought she could have done much. He didn't blame her for what had happened. It would have taken more than simple precautions to prevent that particular gang of kidnappers from taking their target. As it turned out, the gang had been led by a practitioner — a professional kidnapper. Even if Leonie had followed his instructions to the letter, it wouldn't have made much difference. They would have found a way to get her, no doubt about it.

But he could see now how his attitude had contributed to their difficulties. No wonder Holly had torn a strip off him. He'd tried to use the same approach on her, and she had recognised it as the patronising and inappropriate attitude of an overprotective parent to their offspring. *'You'll tell me,'* he'd said arrogantly, and she'd been right. It did show a lack of respect, a lack of awareness that people had their own autonomy and were capable of making their own independent decisions. Shame washed through him at his behaviour. He had behaved like an autocrat. Suddenly, he didn't like himself very much.

He took a deep swallow of his wine as he thought about what to do with his newfound insight. First, he thought, he needed to say he was sorry again to Holly. It was apparent from the expression in her eyes when he'd apologised that she hadn't believed it was genuine. He needed to make sure that she knew he had listened and taken her words on board. And as for Leonie? Well, going forward, he would make sure his attitude was different. He would give her freedom to make her own choices. And hopefully, she would see from that that things had changed.

He tuned back into the conversation just in time to hear Leonie say wistfully, "Oh, you're so lucky to have an imagination like that. I'd love to be able to write a book."

Holly smiled gently at his younger sister and he realised with a jolt that she must have engineered the conversation to get to this point.

"Really?" Holly said. "It's a lot of hard work. Do you like writing yourself?"

"Oh yes, I love it. I... I'm not very good, though."

Holly nodded. "I remember feeling like that. I still do. It's hard to feel satisfied with what you write. It never comes out on paper exactly as you imagined it in your head."

"That's it exactly!" Leonie exclaimed. "It's so frustrating!"

Holly shrugged. "You just have to keep going. You get better as you go along. Actually, Mac was kind enough to say I could stay here for a couple of weeks — both to meet you and to do some writing. My kitchen is—ah—currently being remodelled, and he thought the island might be a good place to work."

Leonie's mouth dropped open. "You're going to write some of the next *Wayfarer* novel here? Oh, that's amazing!"

Holly grinned. "I'd appreciate your help. I need to work out who you are in the story. I'd quite like to write some aspects of your personality into the character as well as your name, if you're up for it."

"*Really*?" Leonie looked utterly astounded.

Mac was, too. He'd had no idea she was going to suggest such a thing. It certainly hadn't been on offer at the auction. But he could see what Holly was doing. If Leonie wanted to be portrayed in the book, she was going to have to stay alive to help her create the character. It was a clever, clever plan.

A sudden tide of gratitude and warmth swept over him as he looked at her, gorgeous in the flickering candlelight. He didn't doubt that by making such a generous offer, she was increasing her own workload exponentially. He dreaded to think how difficult it would be to create a character based upon a real person, especially if they were supposed to act as the real person would in those circumstances. It would be a huge challenge.

Holly shrugged. "Sure. And if you've got anything you've written yourself, I'd be very happy to take a look at it for you, as well."

"Oh! Well, if you're sure..."

It was beautifully done. The way she'd casually dropped the offer of supporting Leonie with her writing appeared entirely unpremeditated. If he hadn't discussed it with her beforehand, he would never have known that Holly was playing out a deliberate strategy.

And that gave him pause, because it showed that she was capable of putting on a convincing front that completely masked her true feelings or intentions.

He absently speared a carrot. She was all smoke and mirrors, this woman, a guarded person who gave little of herself away. But why? Was it because of the thing she didn't want to talk about?

He dreaded to think what *that* was. The look he'd seen on her face wasn't one he ever wanted to see there again.

Glancing up, his eyes met hers, and he received an unpleasant jolt. Her expression was opaque, impenetrable, unreadable. With a sinking feeling, he realised that she'd cut him off, shut him out. He'd pushed her too far in their earlier conversation, and now her barriers were well and truly up.

He should let them stay there, he thought savagely. It would make it easier for them to keep their distance. But damn, he didn't want to. He didn't bloody like this coldness between them, and he sure as hell didn't like that they were so at odds. For better or worse, he needed to talk to her and put things right.

But it didn't turn out to be as easy as that.

Following the meal, Holly excused herself, pleading the need for an early night. And the next morning when he arrived at breakfast, she was deep in conversation with Leonie.

* * * *

Two weeks later, she was still finding excuses to avoid him, and he still hadn't had a chance to talk to her. It was obvious that she was lying low and it was driving him nuts.

They'd had a very brief conversation when Jenna had contacted them to say that they were still no further forward on finding whoever had mailed the rat.

Following the call, Mac tried to talk to Holly about how she was feeling, but she'd just given him a brief shrug before excusing herself to go to the bathroom.

She hadn't returned afterwards.

Since then, the household had fallen into a routine, dividing their time between work and trips out. Holly and Leonie were writing in earnest. Holly seemed to be on a roll, and Leonie had started a story of her own. They were spending hours closeted together in the study, which didn't make getting near Holly any easier.

They'd also had some gorgeous days out. They'd sailed around the Bishop Rock lighthouse and watched the seals and puffins bask in the sunshine. They'd visited the Tresco Abbey Gardens and the Valhalla Figureheads Museum. They'd wandered around Hugh Town and had cream teas in Star Castle. Mac loved watching Holly, who was easily pleased and seemed to take a childlike delight in everything.

"Haven't you ever seen a seal before?" he asked Holly as she took what must have been her thousandth photo of the friendly creatures playing in the water around the boat they were in.

But she just smiled and shook her head before being distracted by a seal pup who had come to investigate the boat. And that was darned near as much as she'd spoken to him. At every turn, she'd evaded him, sticking close to Leonie and James, although he occasionally caught a fleeting glimpse of her looking at him. Sometimes he thought he saw the same longing in her expression that he felt in his own heart, but it was always quickly veiled. She persisted in treating him with an impersonal, distant, friendly politeness that made him want to throw things.

Granted, it didn't help that he was so attracted to her that he couldn't think straight. Every time she walked downstairs in a pair of shorts or a little vest top, he had to stop himself from groaning out loud. He seemed to be in a permanent state of discomfort and the constant hollow ache and vivid, feverish dreams that fragmented his sleep damn near had him on his knees.

Things came to a head one afternoon. When Leonie had been kidnapped, his working life had come to an abrupt halt. He hadn't been able or willing to focus on anything other than getting her back. Everything had been swept to one side. Work had come at the bottom of a very long list of priorities.

But now she was back, and contract deadlines were looming — with penalties attached if he didn't get things finished. A whole mountain of conflicting demands was piling on the pressure, and he couldn't think worth a damn. Every time he sat down and tried to focus, his thoughts went to Holly.

She was haunting him. The discord between them was making him edgy and irritable. He couldn't concentrate on what he was doing and he didn't know what the hell was the matter with him. He'd never been like this before. But he was quickly discovering that being at odds with Holly was having a serious detrimental effect on his output.

Throwing down his pen, he decided he was going to find her and sort things out once and for all. He couldn't stand all this pussyfooting around. It wasn't the kind of man he was. He tackled problems head on. He didn't ignore them while they built up from molehills to mountains.

He found her, predictably, in the study, where she was working with Leonie. As he approached the room, he could hear them discussing Drake. Mac had been shocked to discover, over dinner one night, that Holly intended to have Drake kidnapped in this book—with Leonie's blessing, as it turned out.

It was, as James had said to him later the previous night over a post-prandial brandy, a smart move on Holly's part to include a kidnapping in the plot, as it gave Leonie an indirect way to talk about her experiences. Indeed, the two women had discussed in detail how Drake might react to the shock of being taken, how he might feel whilst being held and the coping strategies he might employ to stay sane and alert under such immense pressure. Now, they were moving on to how he might react once he'd been rescued.

About to knock at the door, he hesitated as he heard Leonie's thoughtful voice say, "I think... I think Drake will back off from Isabella after he's been rescued by her."

He frowned. Why would Drake do that? Holly's reply sounded equally uncertain. "Why? Do you think he'll feel diminished by being rescued by a woman? Because—"

"No, not that." Leonie paused. "Actually, I've always thought that Isabella and Drake's relationship is pretty equal. They're both fiery characters. I can't see Drake being that misogynistic—"

"No. I don't think he would be. So—why might he back off?"

There was a long pause, then Leonie's muffled voice replied, "Because...he'll be ashamed."

Holly's voice was cautious as she asked, "Because he's supposed to be powerful, but…he's been a victim of kidnap?"

"No…because it was his fault!" Leonie's sharp words exploded out of her with all the force of a bullet from a gun.

"*What*?"

"It was his fault! He'll blame himself. Don't you see that? He goes to a market where he *knows* it's dangerous to be alone. He's been warned already. He doesn't take a guide or anyone to back him up and he's taken because he was blindly, criminally, stupidly foolish!"

Silence. Mac felt as if he'd been thrown into an icy lake. Chilled, he heard the pain in Leonie's words and understood at last part of what was stopping his sister from recovering from her ordeal. She blamed herself.

She blamed herself for being kidnapped. And he had never thought to tell her that it wasn't her fault.

If anyone was blindly, criminally, stupidly foolish, it was him.

Holly's next words came as a shock. "Leonie…are you the kind of person who believes that if a woman wears a revealing dress, she deserves to be raped?"

"I — What? No. Of course not! Holly, what the hell?"

Mac was with her on that. *What the bloody hell?*

He heard Holly's voice now, hard and inflexible. "Well, that's what you're insinuating, isn't it? A woman uses her freedom to go where she wants — to do what she wants, to dress how she wants — and she deserves to be trapped, kidnapped, raped?"

"I — No!"

Holly's chair scraped back and Mac heard her heels on the polished oak floor as she walked towards the window to look out at the sea. Her voice was low as she said, "Yes. You're saying Drake deserved to be kidnapped? That he deserved to have his freedom taken away? That he deserved to be held, abused, punished…because he walked through a market?"

"I… Well, I…"

There was a measure of anguish that Mac didn't understand in Holly's voice as she said "People act according to their character, their needs, their personalities. Drake was feeling trapped, hemmed in by people, desperate for some space because of who he is…a loner. He likes company sometimes, but at others he craves solitude. He took the risk and went because he had no choice, because he needed room to breathe, because he was *compelled*."

"Okay…"

He heard a glass clink and the sound of liquid being poured. "Want one?" Holly asked.

"Yes. Brandy."

Another glass was poured, then Holly said evenly, "So what about you, Leonie? People act according to their character. You blame Drake for being kidnapped. What about you? Do you blame yourself? What happened when you were taken, Leonie?"

He heard Leonie's indrawn breath in time with his own. It was a sucker-punch of a question.

"I—" Leonie's voice was choked. He heard her hesitate, then say, "I was in a car, a soft top with the roof down, music blaring. I'd been to Brighton for the day. I drove back into London…towards the city centre and home. I turned into the mews where I live. There was a car blocking it…and another behind…and there were men with balaclavas. It was so quick. I didn't even realise until the ones behind me were out of the car. They just grabbed me, dragged me out…"

The tears Mac could hear in her voice just killed him. He slumped against the wall. She had never talked to him like this.

But Holly was implacable as she asked, "Why, Leonie? You'd been told not to drive around with the roof down, hadn't you? Not to have your music on so loud that you couldn't hear?"

Mac straightened. He'd never told Holly that. She must have heard it herself, the standard advice on how to avoid being kidnapped, and guessed that he would have told Leonie.

With a jolt he realised that as a rich, successful woman herself, Holly was every bit as much at risk of kidnapping as any of his family. Had she, like him, accepted that as an unfortunate side effect of a successful high-profile career and taken precautions as a matter of course? Perhaps she was as acutely aware of the risks as he was.

"I-I..." He heard Leonie stammer.

"*Why*, Leonie? *Why* did you do it? You knew you shouldn't, so why did you?"

"Damn it, because I needed to!" He heard a chair clatter and something smash against a wall. Leonie had thrown her glass, he thought, with considerable force.

"Why?" Holly's voice was fierce. "*Why*?"

"Holly... Oh, Holly...because...I was angry. I was *so* angry... I hated the world and I hated myself. I just didn't care anymore!"

There was a stark silence. Mac felt like every muscle in his body was knotted. To hear that his sister had felt like that... He'd thought she'd been happy in London. He'd had no idea...

"Freedom, Holly," Leonie said bleakly. "I'm like Drake. I need freedom. I was sick of feeling trapped.

Mac's a wonderful brother. I love him more than I could ever tell you, and when we were children, he looked after me, almost like a parent. But he's found it hard to let go since I got older. I moved to London. I wanted to make my own way, but he found me the apartment I have now. And the day before the kidnapping, I discovered that the concierge of the building, Fred, was in touch with Mac, telling him how I was getting on. I felt spied on, betrayed..."

Mac flinched. He'd never imagined anything like this, never. He had never asked Fred to update him on Leonie, though he had once jokingly said, *'Keep in touch.'* He could only guess that Fred, who had two grown-up daughters of his own, had taken that as a request to keep a fatherly eye on her. It was true he did get the occasional e-mail from the older man, but he'd never thought anything of it. He swallowed hard, wishing he too had a brandy in his hand.

"So... so I went to Brighton to see my boyfriend, Alex. I just wanted someone to talk to."

Wait! Leonie had a *boyfriend*?

"I turned up unexpectedly."

Mac's heart plummeted.

"And I found him there...not alone. I came back to London, and I was so full of hell, so upset. I was trying to block it all out with speed...and the sunroof down...and music blasting... And, well, you know what happened then."

"Yes."

"But you know what the worst thing is?"

Mac braced himself. There was *worse*?

"The worst thing is Mac. Since I've been back, he's never, ever said he blamed me. Never asked why I was so stupid, even though he'd *told* me to be careful. But I know he's thinking it. Blaming me. He must be. All this trouble... And he had to borrow so much money at an obscene rate of interest just to get the ransom together in case they couldn't find me. He was going to pay millions, everything he had. It would have ruined him. And even though he didn't pay the ransom, he's paid so much money for me to be in your book...and I don't deserve it. He must be so angry. He must hate me. And now he thinks I tried to kill myself. I saw the pain I caused him in his eyes, and I can't bear it."

He couldn't think, couldn't breathe. Leonie, his precious sister, thought he was angry with her, that he *hated* her?

"No." Holly's dispassionate voice was the calm in the storm. "You're a grown woman. You have a right to your own freedom and independence. If Mac asked someone to watch over you, he was wrong, and you were entitled to object."

Well, at least she'd said 'if' —

"You felt betrayed twice over — by Mac *and* your boyfriend. Naturally, you were upset. Naturally, you looked for ways to let off steam...as you are free to do. Then you were taken. Whose fault was it?"

"But I —"

"Whose fault was it, Leonie?"

"I —"

"*Whose* fault was it?"

"It was *theirs*!" He heard Leonie give a sob, a hiccup. Then there was a sound of a nose being blown and a sigh. Then he heard her say resignedly, "Okay. Yes. It was theirs. The kidnappers. Their fault, not mine."

"Yes. Not yours. You were innocent, and they shouldn't have done that to you."

"No, they shouldn't."

Mac wiped a shaky hand over his damp face. He could hear the belief, the acceptance, in Leonie's voice. She had needed someone to tell her that.

Holly's quiet voice broke into his thoughts. "And what's more, I'd bet good money that Mac doesn't see it as your fault either."

"You...would?"

Of *course* he didn't.

"I would," he heard Holly say, firmly. "You thought Mac would blame you because you were blaming yourself. He doesn't. He may be angry at what the kidnappers did, but he's not angry at you."

No, he damn well wasn't.

"I hope you're right."

"And as for spending money to get you in this book, if you don't respect his right to make independent decisions about his spending, how can you complain if he doesn't respect your right to independence?"

Silence. Then Leonie sighed. "Fair point."

He heard the misery and distress in Leonie's soft voice and couldn't take it anymore. Without a moment's further thought, he shoved open the door.

"Leonie—"

"Mac!" Leonie's cry was shocked. She went to push past him, to get out—

"Oh, hell, no." He caught her arm and swung her round into a hug she wasn't going to get out of any time soon. Burying his face in her hair, he kissed the top of her head and breathed in her precious scent. He felt her tremble, heard a muted snuffle against his shoulder.

He squeezed his eyes closed. If Holly hadn't triggered this conversation, he would never have known how Leonie was feeling. And why not? Because he'd become the kind of man who told, rather than listened. Well, no more. *No more*. He breathed deeply and whispered, "Leonie, just…let me hug you. Please. You're safe, you're here and I love you. I never blamed you, I don't hate you and never *ever* thought it was your fault. How could you think that?"

"Mac, I'm sorry."

"No." He shook his head. "You have nothing to be sorry for. I rather think Holly made that point."

He glanced over at Holly, surprising an expression on her face that he was sure she had not wanted him to see. It was a look of yearning wistfulness mixed with hope and warmth and…love? It quickly turned to shock as she realised he was looking at her, and she instantly replaced it with a bland, neutral smile.

"Even so —"

"It wasn't your fault," he said before dropping a kiss on Leonie's hair then looking up again at Holly. But true to form, she'd slipped out of the room. Of course she had. He was in it. And he *still* hadn't managed to talk to her.

He held his sister in his arms and closed his eyes. He would talk with Leonie, set things straight. Apologise and explain. Make some agreements for the future. He knew in his heart of hearts now that they had got to the root of things, she would start to recover. It would be a long road, but together they would get there.

It was Holly who had done this. Holly who had achieved the impossible — giving his sister the will to live, discovering what was the matter, showing *him* where he had been going wrong. He was so grateful, and so in awe of her perspicacity. She was an amazing woman.

But he was keenly aware that gratitude was not the first emotion that came to mind when he thought of

Holly—nor was passion, though he felt it surge through him whenever she was near. Hell, she didn't have to be near. Whenever he thought about her—which was all the time—what he felt was stronger, purer, more powerful than that.

Emily had betrayed him in the worst way possible and had hurt him to such a degree that he'd thought he could never recover.

But for Holly, he could.

Because he was sure, absolutely sure that Holly would never deliberately hurt him…or anyone else. She was kind. She was clever. And he'd stake his life on the certainty that he could trust her.

His heart lightened, and sudden optimism blossomed in him. He could heal his relationship with Leonie. He could get together with Holly. No longer did his future stretch before him like a barren wasteland.

He could be happy.

They could be happy.

He just needed to convince her of that.

Chapter Seven

Holly was still running from him.

That afternoon, he talked with Leonie for hours. They were honest and open, and he got to know his sister the adult, rather than his sister the teenager. They talked about his over-protective instincts and her need for freedom. They talked about their parents, the business and their hopes for the future.

Leonie smiled shyly at him. "I'm sorry I didn't tell you about Alex," she said.

"Alex?"

"My ex-boyfriend...the rat. I was afraid you might play the heavy big brother and disapprove. He had tattoos...and he was a cage fighter in his spare time."

Mac's eyebrows shot up. "*Really*?"

Laughing, Leonie admitted, "No, not really. Only teasing. Well, he did have the tattoos...but he was actually a bouncer."

"Oh, well, that's all right then," he said, dryly. *A bouncer? Hell.* "Listen... I'm sorry if I ever made you feel

I would disapprove of your choices. I promise that from now on I'll do my best only to give my opinion or advice if I'm asked for it."

"Okay."

"And about your concierge Fred... As I said, I really didn't ask him to report on you, but he does send me emails now and again. I'll show them to you. They don't really say anything about what you're doing, but I'll ask him to stop sending them."

"No. If you didn't ask him then that's enough for me."

"Even so, I'm sorry."

Leonie shook her head impatiently. "Okay, that's enough of the humility now, big brother. I do still value your views, you know. And that being the case... What do you think of James?"

"Not my type," he answered promptly.

"Idiot!" She paused. "No, really..."

Mac looked at her and smiled. "You like him?"

"Mmm."

"He...ah...feels the same way?"

She raised an awkward shoulder. "He hasn't said anything, but I think...maybe."

"He's a good man. You could do worse."

"Yes. I did."

He glanced at her, ruefully. "Ah, well... You don't find your prince without kissing a few frogs first."

She laughed then asked, "What about you? Is Holly *your* princess?"

He looked at his sister then, keenly aware that this was the first personal conversation they'd ever really shared as adults on an even level. "I'd like her to be," he said quietly.

"Ah." Leonie looked at him sympathetically. "You've just got to convince her of that, right?"

"Yes. I think it'll be an uphill battle. I gather she had a bad relationship."

Leonie nodded. "I thought as much. She never talks about her past."

Mac frowned, thinking back over all the conversations they'd had. "No, she really doesn't, does she?" he said slowly.

* * * *

That evening, to his intense frustration, Holly pleaded a headache and didn't come down for supper. The following morning, she was still nowhere to be seen.

James, damn him, noticed. As they sat working in the office after breakfast, he asked wryly, "So, what have you done to upset Holly?"

Mac scowled. "It's my own stupid fault," he muttered. "I pushed her too hard, and now her defences are up."

James raised an eyebrow. "Oh, yes?" he said, mildly.

Deceptively mildly. Mac cast a glance at him and realised what he was thinking. "Not like that!" He shook his head. "The first night she was here, I was talking to her and realised something was bothering her. I…" He grimaced. "I carried on like some Victorian father, demanding she tell me what was wrong."

Amused, James said, "And she told you to back off?"

"Yeah. But I kept on pushing…"

James shook his head. "Well, you'll not make that mistake again."

"No. I'm out in the cold, well and truly."

"She's freezing you off?"

"Mmm. Can't get near her. She's using Leonie as a shield."

"So what were you talking about? You must have struck a real nerve. Holly's pretty self-contained, normally."

That gave Mac pause. James was right. What *had* caused that look on her face? He cast his mind back. "We were talking about Leonie, about how she didn't want to talk about the kidnapping, and she just got this look of—I don't know—horror? Fear? Whatever it was, it shocked me enough that I made a right hash of talking to her about it."

Thinking it over, James asked "What do you know of Holly's past, Mac?"

"Not much. She plays her cards close to her chest. Leonie says she doesn't talk to her about it, either."

James' eyes narrowed, assessing. "You said someone sent her a dead rat? And the police are dealing with it?"

"Yes."

"I think I'll make some enquiries. I don't like it. Something's off. I'll contact the detective you mentioned and offer my services."

Mac nodded. It had been two weeks since Jenna had confirmed her lack of progress. Since then, her occasional e-mails had revealed only frustration as she trawled through fan websites, to no avail. It didn't look like the investigation was making any headway at all. But maybe James, with all of Liberty's resources at his disposal, would have better luck.

"Okay," he said, slowly. "Do that. I'll pay for it."

James shook his head. "No, I'll sort it...as a thank you for what she's done for Leonie."

Mac hid a smile. *So, James really does care about Leonie.* "Okay."

James nodded, then said thoughtfully, "I might have an idea about how you can get Holly on her own. I've been thinking that it's about time Leonie went back to London for a visit. She needs to start getting her life back together. She's becoming too dependent on the island. I don't want her to get to the stage where she's too scared to leave it anymore. I must go back for a few days anyway. Things are piling up at work. I thought I'd go tomorrow morning. There's fog forecast by lunchtime and I don't want to get trapped here. How about if I try to talk Leonie into coming with me?"

Mac glanced sharply at the younger man. There was something awkward about his tone.

"Okay," he said, slowly, "if you think she's ready for it."

"I do."

"But?"

He watched as James picked up his pen and twirled it absently between his fingers. He looked uncomfortable.

Mac suddenly had an inkling of what James' problem might be. He said casually, "I...uh...had a chat with Leonie, yesterday. I overheard her talking to Holly and realised we had some things to sort out."

"Yes, I know. Leonie told me."

"Mmm-hmm." Mac paused and waited until the younger man raised his head and looked at him. He caught his gaze and held it. "I told her I would respect her decisions. She's old enough to make her own choices about things."

"Yes."

"I think she'll make good choices."

A muscle pulsed in James' jaw. He said nothing.

Mac smiled faintly. "If you want to, go for it."

The pen fell from James' fingers and landed on the desk with a clatter. "You don't mind?"

Mac shook his head. "Whatever happens between you two is your business. But for what it's worth, you have my blessing."

"Well...thanks."

"You're welcome."

* * * *

Holly sat on the sheltered beach, propped up against a sun-warmed granite boulder worn smooth by wind and rain, and looked out across the Atlantic. It was a blustery day, and tiny whitecaps could be seen cresting far out to sea. Leonie had said that when that happened, it was rough out there, and the seagulls would head towards land. It was true. Shrieking terns and skuas dived and wheeled across the waves but remained close to the island. But here in this sheltered spot, it was warm enough.

It was the first time Holly had had the chance to investigate the island on her own. That morning, James had asked Leonie if she would go with him to London for a few days. He needed to visit his office there, and he wanted to check that Holly's home was all right.

Leonie had bitten her lip and looked deeply apprehensive. She hadn't been back to London since the kidnapping. But James had smiled gently at her and held out his hand.

'I'll look after you,' he'd promised, softly, and Holly had seen in his expression far more than professional concern. She rather thought that Leonie saw it too,

because with a tremulous smile she stood up and took his hand in hers.

'*All right, then,*' she'd said, clearly mustering courage, '*but you're buying lunch!*'

And so they'd taken off. Holly had waved the helicopter away with some misgivings then promptly decided to take the opportunity to explore the island in Leonie's absence.

And if, in doing so, she managed to avoid Mac, all the better.

So here she was. She'd walked a couple of miles, enjoying the wild drama and freedom of moorland and the jagged cliffs, before finding this quiet little cove. Now she rummaged in her bag and pulled out an apple. Sitting back against the warm stone, she bit into the crisp, sweet, almost fizzy-tasting flesh and closed her eyes. *Delicious.* Coloured spots danced beneath her eyelids as the sun stroked over her face and she relaxed.

The walk had given her time to mull over things. She felt reasonably positive that her visit was helping Leonie. She was confiding in her about all sorts of things. She'd talked about her childhood, the loss of her parents and even about Mac's ex-fiancée. Holly had tried to stop her, feeling she was invading Mac's privacy, until she realised that Leonie was blaming herself for their breakup. Then she'd just shut up and listened, knowing the young woman needed to express her feelings. She'd also tried to encourage Leonie to talk to a professional about her kidnapping and knew that Leonie was now giving it some serious consideration.

As she was. Since her conversation with Mac, she had been struggling with her feelings. She had hated hurting Mac by criticising him so bluntly, but she wasn't sure if her reaction suggested that she was weak like her mother or if it was just the natural response to upsetting someone she cared about.

And those struggles had made her realise how much her past was still influencing her present. As much as she hated the thought of excavating memories she usually tried to keep buried, she knew she was going to have to deal with them or risk being haunted by them for the rest of her life.

So, she vowed that when all this was over and she was back home, she was going to see a counsellor. For better or worse, she needed to try to overcome her past.

She wasn't sure how long she'd been drifting when she heard a quiet chuckle. She opened her eyes to find Mac standing over her. Dressed in jeans, a casual shirt and walking boots, with a rucksack slung over one shoulder, he looked rugged and handsome. Her heart sank even as her body quickened.

He sat down beside her, resting his broad shoulders against the warm rock with a murmur of appreciation. "Nice spot you've found here," he said.

"Yes."

"I've been looking for you. I was hoping to wave Leonie and James off, but I got a phone call at just the wrong minute. As soon as I finished, I ran down to see if I could catch you, but you'd already gone."

"Ah. Sorry."

He wriggled, making himself comfortable and closed his eyes. How could he be so relaxed when he made her feel so edgy?

"You've been avoiding me, haven't you?" His tone was easy, casual, but Holly wasn't deceived. She tensed.

"I—" Her first instinct was to deny it, but she caught herself. Why should she? It was true. "Yes," she said, simply.

A laugh rumbled out of him. "That's my Holly. Honest. Anyone else would have lied."

"Well, I can if you want."

"No." He opened his eyes, amused. "So, why the disappearing act? I've been wanting to talk to you since we spoke that first night."

She looked out over the sea, watched as the breakers crashed against the distant rocks. It struck her that the sea, like time, like life, always caused change – the constant pounding imperceptibly but relentlessly shaping and reshaping the land. The land resisted but in the end was forced to change, just as she had been.

She had altered a lot since she'd come here, she realised now. Gradually, she had become more vulnerable to the ebb and flow of emotions around her. She had grown to care about Leonie and Mac and what they thought. Inevitably, that had changed her. It had made her softer, more exposed…

And that was frightening. What was she becoming? Was she becoming weak like her mother?

Suddenly, she understood that she had not been avoiding Mac because she was afraid of the temptation he represented – though that was true, as far as it went. She had been avoiding him because she was upset that she had caused him pain.

And the fact that it had hurt her so much was frightening and meant that she was already too vulnerable to him. She swallowed hard then said quietly, "I…felt bad."

He jerked back. She could see the confusion in his eyes. "About what?"

"I shouldn't have spoken to you like that. I hurt you."

His eyes widened. "I thought you were avoiding me because you hated my guts for being so overbearing!"

"What? No! I...don't like it when you're like that, but I know your intentions are good. It's only because you care." She watched a wave break against the shore. Mac looked thoughtful.

"Holly, speaking out is a good thing," he said, finally. "I want you to be able to tell me the truth, honestly. I don't ever want you to hold back for fear of hurting my feelings."

Holly glanced at him. "Really?"

"Really," he said firmly. "Didn't you learn to speak up when you were a child?"

"Ah, no. I came from a 'children should be seen and not heard' situation."

Mac frowned. "Well, you're not a child now and I want my brave, fierce Holly back. You can say what you like to me, as bluntly as you want, and as long as you're being honest with me, I can take it. I'm a grown man, you know."

She laughed dryly. "Yes, I do know."

The innuendo was unintended, but it was there, nonetheless. For a moment, memories swirled. Then Mac looked down at his hands and said, "And I wanted to tell you I was sorry for being such a jerk. I had no right to push you like that, and I promise I won't ever do it again."

Speechless, Holly stared at him. He had listened to what she'd said and had changed his ways because of it. He wasn't power-crazed and domineering like Anton, nor was he angry at her for speaking her mind. He was reasonable.

Rich and powerful as he was, he *wasn't* like Anton.

She swallowed hard. This whole situation was just impossible. The more she learned about him, the more she liked him. The last two weeks had been torture. She'd felt the pull of his attraction and the powerful need of her own body constantly. She wanted him so much. She'd tried to keep away from him, every moment spent with him a fraught challenge to hide her feelings.

But inevitably, she'd been obliged to spend some time with him. Mealtimes and trips out had been a torment as she tried to conceal her longing from those around her. She had become increasingly alarmed at the inexorable deepening of her emotions. And seeing how he treated others — and her — with respect, good humour and thoughtful consideration, just intensified her overwhelming emotional connection to him.

It was impossible, with the evidence in front of her eyes, not to acknowledge that he was a good man, one who loved his family and those close to him deeply, who would do anything for them, go to any lengths to protect them and ensure they were safe and happy. And if she wished she was one of that charmed circle, enfolded in his love, then she was not going to admit it — to herself or anyone else.

And the nights... Oh, the nights. Not a night went by without her twisting and turning through the long hours of darkness, her body pulsing and aching for fulfilment, unable to prevent the torrent of memories of their agonisingly brief time together.

She took a steadying breath, regretting it when she caught his scent on the wind. Instantly, she was lying next to him in bed, her head resting on his shoulder, breathing in the warm aroma of his skin, replete after...

With a jolt she realised he was speaking to her, and she had no clue what he'd said. "I... Sorry, I —"

Mac gave her a teasing look. "I said, am I forgiven?"

"Oh! Yes. Of course. If I am, that is..."

"There's nothing to forgive," he said. "You were speaking your mind, and I thank you for it. Hard though it is to believe" — he smiled crookedly — "I do sometimes need someone to point out where I'm going wrong."

"Ah, well," she said without thinking, "I'm your woman, then."

"I wish you were."

There was a long, tense silence. Then Holly said diffidently, "It's okay. I understand why...why you don't really want to get involved."

He raised his eyebrows. "You do?"

She nodded. "Leonie told me...about Emily."

There was no mistaking the astonishment in his eyes. "She did? I'm surprised she remembers much about it. She was only thirteen."

Holly nodded. "She seems to recall it clearly. I think she blames herself for you losing the love of your life."

"*What?*"

"She said Emily left you because you were saddled with a little sister to look after."

Mac stared, then shook his head ruefully. "I've been such an idiot," he said. "I should have talked to her about Emily long before this. Emily didn't leave me because of Leonie."

"She...didn't?"

"Nope." He sighed. He really didn't want to think of Emily, but it looked as if he was going to have to. "Emily left because she was pregnant."

"*What?*"

He sighed. "She told me she was pregnant about a month before my parents died. I was surprised. We'd been taking precautions, but I know that sometimes things go amiss. Anyway, I had a good job working for my father's firm, so I thought we'd be all right. And I was so excited at the idea of being a father." He laughed softly. "I was only nineteen myself, just a kid still, really. Anyway, we decided not to tell anyone until the first trimester was over. She was superstitious about that kind of thing."

Holly nodded. She knew lots of people waited until the first three months were up before telling people.

He took a deep breath and looked down at the heather at his feet. "Just before we were going to tell them, my parents were killed. A drunk driver." He ran a rough hand through his hair. "It was touch and go whether the business would survive without my father at the helm. For a while, it looked like the money would run out and we would have to declare bankruptcy."

He looked up, staring out over the sea. "That was when she told me. The baby wasn't mine. Whilst I'd looked like the better bet financially, she'd been going to stay with me. When she thought I was going to lose everything, she went to live with the father of her baby."

Holly felt her mouth drop open. "That's awful. Mac, I'm so sorry."

"No. Don't be. She's happy with the man she went to, and I still see their little boy occasionally on St. Mary's. And whilst a part of me still mourns the child I thought I was going to have, another part of me knows that I had a lucky escape. I could have married her never knowing that she'd cheated or that the child I was raising wasn't mine." He sighed. "I'll admit I was devastated when I found out. It left me with a real mistrust of women. After that, I swore never to get closely involved with anyone again."

"So…you're not still in love with her?"

"Hell, no!" He slanted her a wry grin. "And I think my mistrust of women has abated a little, since I met you. You're the real deal."

She stared at him, suddenly feeling a confusing mixture of anxiety and excitement. Was he trying to say he wanted her as a partner? Did he want a *relationship*? Things might have changed from his perspective, but they hadn't from hers. She couldn't get involved with him. She couldn't. True, she had realised that he wasn't as controlling and overbearing as Anton, but he was still a man of huge power and influence.

But he would never use that power against me.

The thought came to her suddenly but with absolute certainty. She had seen how he had acted these last few weeks, how he'd dealt with other people, how he'd coped with being challenged. He might not like it when people disagreed with him, but he listened and took criticism on board.

She thought about how he'd been on their first night together. *'You'll not come to any harm with me.'*

She hadn't fully believed him then. She did now.

So what was standing in her way?

Her past. Her past was standing in the way. There was no way she would ever tell Mac about it. It was too horrible.

Nor could she lie about it. What kind of real relationship could she build without honesty? It would be impossible to move forward whilst hiding so much of her history. Inevitably, he would ask questions, and inevitably, her refusal to answer would drive a barrier between them.

But then, he hadn't asked her to have a full relationship with him, had he? What had he said? *'There's nothing stopping us from getting together.'* Perhaps, she thought with dawning optimism, he just meant sexually.

Could she handle them having a purely physical relationship? Not one night of pleasure but many, without getting more deeply drawn in emotionally?

Her instincts warned her that she couldn't. She was already in too deep. But her body and her desire and her emotions said yes. They wanted her to grasp at the opportunity for one more time with him — or as many times as she could get. He was special, precious, wonderful and if she could only have him for a short time, then she should.

She would regret it forever if she didn't. But she might be devastated by his loss for the rest of her life if she did.

A random line from Andrew Marvell popped into her thoughts and she wondered absently if Mac knew it.

Tear our pleasures with rough strife through the iron gates of life...

The poet had declared it thus, and he was right. Time was short and no one was promised another day. It was the wisdom of ages to grab pleasure when the opportunity arose. Who was she to argue with such a sentiment?

She had no illusions. Her mind was throwing up such quotes to justify what she wanted to do, even though she knew she shouldn't.

The iron gates would close soon enough on their relationship. She should take what was offered and tear the pleasure from it.

She swallowed. Still unsure what he wanted from her, she said cautiously, "Mac, I... I can't promise anything."

He shook his head. "I'm not asking you to."

"I don't... I don't want to get in too deep."

She wouldn't allow herself to give in to love. She wouldn't. Emotional distance... That was the key.

His expression was opaque, unreadable. His grasp on her hands tightened. "I've told you before that we go exactly as far as you want and no further. It'll be all right, Holly."

She looked into his eyes then, his piercing blue eyes, and felt the heat in his gaze fizz through her like champagne. A wild, riotous, giddy froth of sudden happiness surged through her. "All right, then," she said, throwing caution to the wind. For once in her life, she was going to take her pleasure and to hell with the consequences. "For better or worse... Let's do it!"

Chapter Eight

Do what? he thought, darkly.

He had no illusions that right now she was talking about making love. She was promising nothing more than physical intimacy. He had seen her hesitation, her fear of more in her expressive face. But what was holding her back?

Her ex had been cruel. That much was clear. But she must know that he wasn't like that. Their night together must have proved it, and surely their time together since then must have shown her that he was no threat. And she was attracted to him. He had seen the emotion in her eyes more than once. She wanted him. Sometimes, when she didn't realise he was watching her, he even thought he could see love mingled with that wanting. But that could be wishful thinking on his part.

His heart twisted. He hoped he wasn't imagining it. If she did feel love for him but was just afraid for some reason, then he needed to find out what the problem was and overcome it. His life, his future... Everything depended on it. He wanted so much more than just her body. He wanted *everything*—a relationship, love... *marriage*?

Marriage. The very word jolted him.

Since Emily, he'd always shied away from the thought, the idea. But now it wrapped around him like a soft, warm blanket. Marriage with Holly... It felt perfectly right. They belonged together. He had no doubt, none at all, that she was the only woman he would ever want as his wife.

His love for her shone clearly inside him, diamond-bright. He could *feel* its power, its beauty. There were no shadows, no doubts. He knew absolutely that she was the one.

If she would have him.

It scared him that she was pulling the other way. *'I don't want to get in too deep,'* she'd said, when he wanted the opposite. He dreaded to think how he would feel if he couldn't change her mind.

But he had to think positively. There was hope. At least she'd agreed to engage with him on some level. It was up to him now to capitalise on that. He would start where she wanted to—with a physical connection. Goodness knew he wanted that, too. But he would build on it, try to strengthen the bonds of feeling between them.

Moving away a strand of hair that swept across her face in the light breeze, he asked, "Here? Now?"

A gasp, a startled laugh. He'd shocked her.

"Too public?"

She assessed their surroundings. Behind them, they were shielded by the huge granite rocks and in front of them nothing but sand and sea.

He nodded out at the ocean. "There's nothing out there for five thousand miles until you hit South America."

"Hmm. A bit close, then." Her lips twitched and he laughed.

"If you're uncomfortable, we'll go home. It's okay."

"Oh, no. Here's good." He watched a blush blossom on her cheeks and hid a smile. For all her confidence, she could sometimes be a little shy.

He remembered with pleasure that she'd once said she'd like to make love on a beach. She'd said she'd like to try it in the sea as well, but the ocean here was too cold for that. Maybe he'd persuade her to go with him to somewhere where the water was warm. Fiji... Or there was a gorgeous island just off Bali that she would really love, where they could fulfil that particular dream. It would be a great place for a honeymoon.

His body throbbed at the thought of it, and he turned hastily away from her observant gaze to rummage in his bag for a picnic blanket.

Her eyebrows arched. "You came prepared?"

"Only for a picnic. I persuaded Flora to pack lunch. There's more stuff in this rucksack than in Hermione's handbag."

"'*Hermione's handbag*?' You're a Potter fan?"

He laughed. "Of course. I watched them all with Leonie as she was growing up. How about you?"

"I read them as an adult."

He spread the blanket on the sand. "You haven't seen the films?"

"No."

"Hmm." He lay down and held his arm out to her. "Well, maybe we should create some magic of our own."

"Okay… You want to warm up your wand?" she asked insouciantly.

Damn, she was wicked. Wicked and wonderful. And if she knew how hot his wand really was, she wouldn't be so blasé about it. Laughing out loud, he replied, "Not to be too presumptuous, but I was rather hoping you would do that."

Chuckling, she settled down beside him, resting her head on his arm. She was a little awkward, a little tense, as she snuggled into his side. But he couldn't help but sigh with contentment. She felt just right tucked in beside him. She belonged there.

They lay like that for a while, enjoying being together, watching the soft clouds drift overhead. He desperately wanted to grab her, to take her with all the fierce, savage passion that flamed in him, to pour out his love and frustration in one wild, explosive act of lovemaking. He wanted to, but he wasn't going to do that.

Because, beyond his own needs, his own agonising cravings, his instincts were telling him in no uncertain terms that she needed time to adjust to their newfound accord, time to relax, to feel comfortable with him again. And so he lay still, staring at the sky, trying to control his raging heartbeat and blazing arousal.

Gradually, her body softened. After a while, she exhaled softly, and her warm breath tickled his neck. The sensation ran through him like electricity, and it was all he could do to hide his reaction from her. Restless warmth pooled in his groin. He wondered if the same thing was happening to her. When her warm hand slid tentatively over his waist, he took it as a sign that she might be ready and rolled onto his side to face her.

She was, thank goodness. He couldn't have held out much longer. Her eyes were wide, her pupils dilated and her breathing shallow. A full flush ran along her cheek bones.

Gently, he said, "I promised you on your first day on the island that I wouldn't touch you again."

Her eyes flickered anxiously. "You'll break your promise?"

"You'll allow me to?"

There was relief then tenderness in her expression. She reached up and stroked his face. He had a momentary random thought that he was glad he'd shaved so he was smooth for her, before her tiny, breathy answer drove everything out of his mind.

"Yes."

His breath caught. Slowly, softly, he stroked his thumb over her lips. "I can touch you here?" he whispered. The contact jolted him. He'd missed that so much. The last fortnight had seemed like an eternity.

Her lips parted and quivered beneath his thumb.

Slowly, lightly, he kissed her with gentle butterfly kisses until she reached up around him in frustration to pull his head down. He deepened the contact then, letting his tongue dance and play with hers until they were both breathless and dizzy.

He was as hard as a rock, but he resisted the urge to move faster, to strip her and take her right here, right now, with the wild ocean crashing against the rocks nearby.

No. No. He wanted to stretch out the moment, to make it last forever, to give her every ounce of pleasure he could. She'd been deprived by her previous lover. She would not be short-changed by him.

He lifted his head to look at her. With satisfaction, he saw that she looked glazed and heavy-lidded with passion, ripe and faintly desperate for more. With the lightest of touches, he feathered his fingers over the tender skin revealed by the vee of her shirt.

"And here," he said, quietly. "May I touch you here?"

"Oh, yes."

The words were nothing more than a murmur. Unhurriedly, he unbuttoned her top and stroked open the soft fabric. She was wearing a simple, pretty bra — white, with a touch of lace. It displayed the delicious curve of her breasts in a way that made him want to groan.

He *was* groaning. Belatedly, he became aware of the fact and glanced up at Holly's face to see if she'd registered the sound.

She had. Of course, she had. She was watching him look at her. He smiled. "You're so damn lovely," he said. "I don't know how to contain myself." But contain himself he did, drifting his fingers over her sensitive skin until she writhed and twisted, then used his mouth to drive her to even greater need. He breathed in the heady scent of roses from her skin, tasted her light, musky fragrance and his head spun.

His hand strayed to the waistband of her jeans. He looked at her again. "And may I...? May I...?" He touched the button and she nodded.

He rose onto his knees and took off her boots and socks, then slid the soft denim down her long legs. She was wearing tiny panties again — white and silky this time. Innocence and sexiness. *Pretty.*

She rested her feet in his lap and he rubbed them with circular movements that he was amused to see made her stretch out like a little cat. Soon, her body was moving sinuously in time with his fingers, and her eyes were closed.

He massaged her instep and her ankles then moved up to her calves, her knees, her inner thighs...

She was aroused now, releasing panting breaths, and there was tension in the muscles beneath the silky skin. She was so beautiful.

He edged closer then deliberately skimmed his thumbs over the soft, damp silk of her panties. She arched, crying out at the sudden flash of sensation. He pressed his thumbs more deeply, drawing lazy circles over the tender flesh, and she writhed.

"Mac, please!"

She was ready...more than ready. Another minute and she would be there, but he wanted to be inside her when that happened.

He drew back to grab his wallet from his pocket, then fumbled to unzip his own jeans. His damn hands were shaking so badly that he could hardly unfasten them. He thrust them down, yanked his boots, boxers, shirt...everything off. He wanted nothing between them, nothing at all. The warm air stroked against vulnerable skin and he shook with sensation. Falling to his knees, he returned to caress her once more. She moaned.

Oh, he loved her like this, eyes closed, so abandoned, so close to the edge...

There was a condom — thankfully — in his wallet and he rolled it on with such alacrity that he didn't realise Holly had opened her eyes and was watching him until he heard her laugh. He looked up and grinned ruefully. "I think I broke the world speed record there — " Then his gaze landed on her pretty breasts and all humour was forgotten. "Holly," he said thickly, leaning towards her.

But she sat up and drew him down beside her, so they lay side by side facing each other. "Mac," she said softly.

Unable to hold out another minute, he pulled her close. That bra had to come off. He had to feel her skin against his. He didn't realise he'd said it out loud until she said, "Take it off, then."

He didn't need telling twice. He had her out of her bra and panties between one breath and the next, then she was wrapped in his arms, pressed against him, skin against skin, and he was kissing her as if his life depended on it.

Her softness pressed against his hardness, and he ran his hand down her back and over the delicious curve of her bottom. She smelled of pure woman, and he knew he couldn't last much longer.

"Please," he gasped, nudging softly against her. He looked at her and saw the same overwhelming need reflected. She moved her leg, just slightly, but it was enough, and he slid inside her with a gasp.

Hauling her tight against him, wrapping his arms round her, he moved deeply within her. His heart felt as if it would burst out of his chest. He thrust a hand in her hair and pulled her head close so he could kiss her.

She kissed him back, her fire matching his. Everything was heat and movement and wildness. He was drowning, he was flying and she was losing it.

Her body writhed in the confines of his arms, and she fought to get closer, to *dance* on him, then suddenly, wildly, she arched, stiffening and crying out in a long wail of pleasure.

And the pressure, the heat and the pulsing tightness of her body embracing his and the glorious sound of her cry shimmering like angel music through him was enough to drive him beyond himself, beyond sanity, beyond the world — he was going to *burst* — and he exploded, catapulted into a heart-stopping hurricane of sensation that never seemed to end.

Chapter Nine

He'd never felt anything like it.

So this is what it feels like with the woman you love.

Afterwards, he held her gasping, trembling body in his arms—kissing, stroking, soothing her. After such intensity, he knew she needed comfort.

Gradually, she relaxed, quieted then settled against him. He kissed her hair and her tummy rumbled.

He laughed. "Was that apple all you've had to eat today?" he asked.

"Yes. I left the house early to go to the helipad."

She'd left the house early to avoid him, and he knew it. James and Leonie hadn't gone that early. But he let it pass.

"How about that picnic now, then?"

"Oh, yes!"

He had to give it to her, Flora had outdone herself with the picnic. She'd packed a delicious meal of bread, assorted cheeses, apples and grapes and had thrown in a thick slab of fruitcake and a bottle of wine. *Perfect.*

They tucked in with gusto, enjoying the creamy cheese, the sweet black grapes, the rich denseness of the cake and the sharpness of the crisp white wine. The fresh, salty sea air added an extra piquancy to the meal.

Afterwards, Holly sighed with satisfaction then blurted, "Mac, what's that over there?"

He glanced where she pointed and saw a low line of clouds on the horizon. Glancing at his watch, he frowned. "It's a fog bank," he replied. "There's one in the forecast, but it's early. We should pack up and head home. When the fog rolls in here, it's usually very thick and heavy."

Five minutes later, they were on their way. Mac held her hand but walked quickly, and she felt quite out of breath by the time they'd arrived back at the house.

They were just in time. The fog descended suddenly within minutes of them reaching home, obscuring everything.

"Wow," Holly said, still catching her breath, staring out of the sitting room window at the swirling, dark mist, "I've never seen fog as dense as that." The glorious view had gone, the pulsing flash of the lighthouse beam cutting through the mist the only sign that the world still existed beyond the windows.

"Yes," said Mac, busy turning on the table lamps. "It can get pretty bad here and lasts for days, sometimes. I'm glad James and Leonie got away before it arrived. Oh, and Flora and Pete have gone, as well. They wanted to go to visit the twins, and when I realised that there was only going to be you and me here, I gave them a few days off. I thought we could fend for ourselves."

Holly's eyebrows shot up. "We're here...on our own?"

Mac turned, suddenly sharply aware of the wariness in her voice. After crossing the room, he took her hands in his. "Holly," he said carefully, "we're safe here. We're geared up for bad weather, and we have our own generator and plenty of supplies. We won't starve."

Her gaze avoided his. That wasn't the problem, so what was? He thought for a minute, looking at his woman who *hated* to be pushed into things...then he knew. He tightened his fingers around hers. "And if you think it'll be different—if you think *I'll* be different when there's no one here, you're wrong. What we did out there on the beach today was lovely, but I don't expect a repeat performance. I don't expect *anything* of you. Right?"

She glanced up at him and grimaced. "Sorry," she said.

He shook his head. "Idiot. Now, this afternoon... Do you want me to leave you in peace to do some writing, or if you like, we could watch a movie?"

After some debate, they decided to watch the first *Harry Potter*. It was clear from the first magical chords that Holly was entranced by the plot, her inner child totally absorbed in the fantastic story. She curled up on the sofa, cuddled up against him and lost herself totally.

Mac, who hadn't seen the films since Leonie was young, enjoyed having Holly in his arms as much as he liked the movie itself. Moreover, he loved watching her reactions. She was rapt, mesmerised by the story, excitement and delight playing across her features as she watched the plot unfold.

He would love to see her at Christmas, he thought. He could just imagine her excitement at decorating the tree or opening presents on Christmas morning. He hoped fervently that she *would* be with him on Christmas Day so he could see it for real.

The movie finished, and she looked at him, pure pleasure in her expression. "Oh, Mac, that was stunning! That poor child, mistreated and alone, rescued and sent somewhere wonderful..."

He smiled down at her. "Would you have liked that?" he probed, casually. "To have been whisked away from your childhood to another life?"

If she hadn't been curled up against him, he would have missed the quickly supressed flinch.

She shrugged lightly and laughed. Was it his imagination, or did it sound a little forced? "Who wouldn't?" she said, casually. "Who could resist the lure of Hogwarts?" She cleared her throat and glanced up at him. "I don't suppose...you fancy watching another one?"

At seven, they stopped for supper. Flora had left them a delicious beef casserole seasoned with thyme and red wine, so they heated it up and ate it at the kitchen table with chunks of crusty bread.

Holly was bubbling over with enthusiasm for the movies and chatted animatedly as they ate. "I loved the wizard chess scene," she said. "I've always wanted to play chess."

Mac laughed. "I'll teach you if you like. There are loads of board games here."

"Really?"

There was excitement in her voice, and he paused mid-forkful. "You like board games?" he asked, curiously.

"I don't know. I've never played any."

"Never?"

"No."

She plainly didn't want him to ask any more, but he couldn't help but wonder. "Okay then. After supper… chess. But I warn you that I'm very competitive. I play to win!"

At midnight, they reached a stalemate. He held up his hands, watching as Holly hid a yawn. "Okay," he said, laughing, "I give up. You're really good at this. I'll not be able to touch you after a few more games!"

Holly sat back and grinned. "Oh, I really loved that," she said, satisfied. "Can we play some more tomorrow?"

He nodded. "Sure. Tomorrow, we should introduce you to the joys of Monopoly. I'd suggest Scrabble, but knowing your way with words, I wouldn't stand a chance!"

They went to bed. Holly, to his intense pleasure, agreed to sleep with him. "We don't have to do anything," he said, as he extended the tentative invitation. "But even if you'd just like to sleep with me…I'd love it."

The expression on her face made it clear that she'd love it, too, and as they switched the lights off and climbed the stairs hand in hand, Mac knew that he wanted to do this with her every night for the rest of their lives.

He took her to his bedroom. She'd never been in it before, and it felt right seeing her there.

She wandered around, familiarising herself with the furnishings, the pictures, and he was suddenly reminded of their first night together. When she'd been nervous…

Clearing his throat, he said, "I forgot— I meant to bring a glass of water up with me. Would you like one, too?"

She glanced at him, blankly. "I…uh, yes. Sure. That would be nice."

He nodded. "There are T-shirts in the top drawer if you want one to sleep in. And the bathroom's through there, if you want to use it," he said casually, and left her to it.

He gave her a good ten minutes before he returned, praying she hadn't changed her mind in the meantime.

But no, she was there, in bed, looking faintly apprehensive.

Did she think he was going to push her to make love, even when he could see she was exhausted? Was that what her ex had done?

He set the water down then pulled a pair of pyjama trousers out of a drawer and headed for the bathroom. He didn't normally wear them, but he had a feeling Holly would feel more comfortable if he did.

When he emerged, she glanced at him then away. "Everything all right?" he asked as he climbed into bed.

"Uh, yes. Fine."

"Alright if I switch the lights out?"

"Sure."

He turned off the lamp and the room fell into darkness. He rolled onto his back and said quietly, "Fancy a hug?"

"Oh!" She gave a small laugh and rolled towards him. He put out his arm and cuddled her into his side. She was wearing one of his T-shirts. He liked it.

"There," he said. "That's better."

She relaxed against him, settled her small hand on his chest. "Mac," she said, softly, "thank you for today. It's been the most perfect, lovely day ever. Earlier, when we were together…then the films and games…"

A laugh rumbled in his chest. No other woman of his acquaintance would have thought it a good day, let alone a perfect one. Most of the women he'd been acquainted with had enjoyed the high life—fine dining, exotic trips, shopping. None, until now, had ever enjoyed a day just for the pleasure of being together. Neither—now that he thought about it—had he.

But with Holly, everything was different. With her, he didn't care what they did, where they went. He just loved being with her.

He smiled. "There are plenty more days where this one came from."

She sighed contentedly. "I hope so."

"I know so." He raised a gentle hand and stroked her hair. "Now go to sleep. It's been a long day and you need your rest."

Her whole body melted trustingly against his. "Okay. G'night."

He smiled in the darkness. "Night, sweetheart."

He lay in the darkness, listening as her breathing deepened into sleep. The day had been a success in lots of ways. He'd finally managed to get her to stop running and talk to him, and they had managed to resolve some of their issues.

He had been shocked when she'd said she felt bad about the way she'd spoken to him. He and Leonie had been raised to express their feelings openly, and they had always been listened to. He wondered how different Holly's childhood must have been for her to be so concerned at his reaction to what had been, in his eyes, nothing more than the expression of a few home truths.

It wasn't as if Holly didn't have form when it came to speaking her mind. She'd certainly told Leonie straight when she'd discovered the younger woman was blaming herself for her kidnapping. But come to think of it, she hadn't come down to dinner or breakfast after that episode. At the time, he'd thought that she was just avoiding him, but now he wondered if she'd been upset at speaking out that way.

It was, he now realised, as if Holly had two sides to her character. The one he saw on a day to day basis was the adult – the mature, successful, perceptive woman, who was able to speak her mind freely and eloquently, especially if she thought it would help those she cared about. But the other side of her was the Holly of the past – the child, who, as far as he could see, was still struggling with the inhibitions and constraints instilled in her in childhood.

He could see that today he'd managed to reassure the woman. Their subsequent lovemaking had proved that. But the child…

He'd seen her inner child quite often. That was the Holly who was so excited at baby seals and castle visits and *Harry Potter*. But it was also the part of her who retreated fast and hid whenever a question was asked. *'Does the candy twist remind you of your childhood?' 'You'd like to have been whisked away to another life?' 'You've never played a board game?'*

Was that younger self afraid of him? Why would she be? He'd never done anything to frighten her – and he never would. But maybe *he* wasn't the problem. Holly had had problems with her ex, he knew, but what if she'd also had problems farther back in the past? His stomach knotted. *What kind of demons is she hiding?*

She stirred in his arms, cuddling more closely into his side. The adult Holly knew she was safe, even in sleep. But he had a grim feeling that he was going to have to overcome Holly's childhood fears and reassure that inner child she was safe, if he was ever to persuade her that he was the one for her.

Chapter Ten

He drifted back into consciousness in the most delicious way possible. One minute he was having a spectacularly erotic dream about Holly touching him, and the next his mind was suddenly aware that the hands stroking his skin were anything but ephemeral.

Keeping his eyes closed and his breathing steady, he lay still as she stroked her slender fingers lightly over his shoulders and down his arms. Returning to his shoulders, she ran them over his ribs and across his chest, pausing to caress the sensitive area around his nipples.

They tightened as she flicked them lightly. She toyed with them for a moment, then, tantalisingly, she moved on. Next, those torturing fingers slid across his stomach, and it was all he could do to stop the muscles from contracting. She drifted lower and he squeezed his eyes shut. In a moment, she was going to touch him and he was going to explode…

To his intense frustration, she suddenly removed her hand and whispered, as if to herself, "No." There was a pause and a light sigh. Then, as soft as thistle down, she said, "Oh, Mac, I wish…"

She trailed off, but the sadness in her tone alarmed him. It was as if there was no hope to be found.

He turned towards her and opened his eyes as if he were just waking. "Morning, gorgeous," he mumbled.

"M…morning."

"Kiss?"

Her eyes widened. "With pleasure," she said, wrapping her arms around him, pulling him close so she could kiss him deeply.

Pressed against her as he was, there was no hiding his arousal. But she didn't seem to mind as she kissed him, thrusting her tongue into his mouth as she moved her body against him, making him gasp.

He slid his hand under the hem of her T-shirt then between her silky thighs. She groaned into his mouth and he realised that her morning explorations had aroused her as much as him.

She was *ready*.

With a moan of pure need, he reached one-handed into his bedside cabinet to grab a condom, pulled it on and, in one fluid motion, rolled her onto her back and moved over her.

Still kissing her, he lowered himself, pressing against the cradle of her hips. She was so warm, so ready. Her body was soft, pliant, musky, welcoming him.

She fluttered her hands against his shoulders…

Then suddenly the little hands bunched and punched his shoulders, she ripped her mouth away from his and a hoarse cry was accompanied by the frantic twisting of her slim body. "Stop!"

Shocked, he rolled off her, unprepared for the way she leapt up and retreated across the bedroom. He scrambled to his feet, feeling shaken, disorientated and not a little horrified. He went after her.

"Don't touch me! Please!" Her voice was shrill. She threw up her hand as if to physically ward him back.

He jerked to a halt.

Her eyes were wild. He didn't suppose his own were much better. *What the hell?*

"Okay. Okay. I won't touch you. I promise. You're safe." He took a slow step back and drew in a shaky breath, shuddering as he fought to control his breathing and the rousing effects of the adrenalin coursing through him.

He'd done something wrong, but what? Had he reminded her of her ex in some awful way? Frightened her? Shit, had he *hurt* her?

He didn't know, but he sure as hell needed to find out.

But first, he needed to calm her down.

"Wait," he said, abruptly. He turned and went quickly into the bathroom, disposed of the condom and pulled on his robe. Somehow, he didn't think that reasoning with her whilst naked was going to do the trick.

After returning to the bedroom, he sat on the edge of the bed. She was still standing exactly where he'd left her. Gathering his thoughts, he said slowly, "Holly... sweetheart... I'm sorry. Did I hurt you?"

She winced, shaking her head.

"Okay," he said slowly, "that's good. Because I wouldn't hurt you for the world. You know that, right?"

"You... You didn't." Her voice was husky. "It wasn't your fault. I... I'm sorry."

Sorry?

"You have nothing to apologise for, Holly. Just tell me what happened."

Please.

He watched her struggle for words, start then stop again. Her shoulders drooped. It was clear that words were eluding her.

"Okay," he said, evenly, though inside he was desperately worried. "Holly, come and sit with me. I won't touch you. I promise."

She hesitated.

"Please. I need you." He held his breath. If he knew one thing about Holly, it was that she was kind. If she believed there was a need, she would try to meet it. It was why she did so much for charity. Why she had gone so far out of her way to help his sister. Would *his* need be enough to sway her?

It was.

With visible reluctance, she sat down beside him. She looked mortified and utterly embarrassed.

How the hell was he going to get her to talk to him? A memory of Leonie, in the early days after her release, drifted into his head. Then, she had found it almost impossible to talk about what had happened to her. Then James had arrived, and he had... What had he done? Yes. He'd used closed questions to break the ice.

"Okay," he said calmly. "I can see you're finding this hard to talk about, sweetheart. So, I'm just going to ask you some questions."

She stiffened.

"You only have to answer yes or no. That's all."

She took a few deep breaths. "Okay."

"Right. First, are you hurt?"

"No. I'm okay."

He was getting more than one-word answers. That was good.

"Did you change your mind? Because you always can, you know. If you say 'no,' at any point, we stop. You don't have to feel bad about that."

"No. I didn't change my mind."

He stared out of the panoramic window. There was nothing but dense fog outside. "We've made love before. You weren't afraid then. So what was different this time?"

She shook her head and jerked impatiently to her feet. He got up quickly. She wasn't running away from this. The last time something had gone wrong between them, he'd had two weeks of her avoiding him. There was no way he was leaving this problem unresolved.

"What is it?" he said, tensely. "Holly, just tell me."

He watched the struggle play out in her eyes and realised that she was waging her own internal war. A part of her, at least, wanted to tell him what was wrong. But something was stopping her. Was the younger, more fearful Holly holding back the adult?

He had no idea if he was right in his theory, but he had nothing better to go on. Making a decision, he decided to talk to the frightened child directly.

"Holly," he said firmly, "look at me."

Reluctantly, her gaze met his. At least she was able to do that. But his heart twisted as he saw her distress.

"Okay, good," he said. "Now, I want you to listen to me. I don't know what scared you just now, but whatever it was, you and I are going to deal with it together. You're not on your own anymore. You don't have to handle everything by yourself. I'm on your side."

There was a long pause, then in a low voice she said, "No. It's too horrible. If I tell you, you'll go." For a moment, she looked startled, as if she couldn't believe she'd spoken such words out loud.

"No, I won't," he said, steadily, though inside he was hurting. She did not want to tell him because she thought he'd *leave* her? "No matter what you tell me, I'll be right here by your side. No matter what. You can trust me. I promise."

A flicker of indecision crossed her features.

"Now," he said evenly, "tell me what this is all about. Tell me everything. Whatever this is, you've carried it too long on your own. Let me take some of the burden from you."

He prayed as he'd never prayed before as she made her decision. He knew that if they were to stand any chance — any chance at all, of building an intimate, loving relationship — she had to trust him not only with her body but also with her secrets. Without that trust, they were lost.

There was a long silence whilst she thought about what he'd said. And he saw the moment in her eyes when the decision was made, when the adult and the child coalesced into one.

"Yes," she said quietly. "Okay...yes."

Relief and gratitude poured through him in equal measure. If she could tell him, there was hope for them. And there was no doubt that her agreement was a massive statement of trust and faith in him.

Exhaling a shaky breath, he took her hand in his. "Good. You won't regret it, sweetheart. Now take your time. I'm listening."

He watched as she squared her shoulders and gathered herself. Her courage was evident and impressive. Finally, she said quietly, "I'm sorry I flipped out on you. I d-don't like that position."

That position? That sexual position? "Me on top, you mean?" he clarified.

"Yes."

Was that why she'd rolled onto her side on the beach? He felt his jaw clench. This didn't sound good, not at all. "This is that bastard again, isn't it? Your ex. What did he do, Holly?"

"It wasn't him."

For a moment, he thought he'd misheard.

As if she'd read his thoughts, she went on, "And he didn't, quite…"

"But someone tried?"

"Yes."

For a moment his vision blurred with fury. "Who?" He would rip him limb from limb. He would *destroy* him.

Her face flamed. "It's a long story."

And he needed to hear it. His voice was unintentionally hard. "I'm listening."

She winced. Clearly, she wished he wasn't. "I was born and raised in a cult, near Edinburgh."

Immediately, a whole lot of things fell into place. No wonder she had never encountered Harry Potter or board games or baby seals.

"I was there until I was thirteen," she went on. "That was the about the age that Anton Devereaux, the leader of the cult, decreed that girls were old enough to get married…to *him*."

A cold, creeping horror ran through him. "He married girls at *thirteen*?"

"Well, there was only me there who was that young. But the rule was once they…once a girl menstruated," she mumbled, "he would be the first husband of each one of them in the cult. He could sleep with anyone he wanted, and no one could stop him. He had punishments for disobedience. It was very strict."

It just kept getting worse.

She gave an awkward shrug. "I never saw my mother with a man. I had always assumed Anton was my father, so I didn't think he would —"

"No."

"When I found out that we were to be married, I appealed to my mother, but she said it would be an h…honour."

Oh, no.

"But one of the guards, Thomas, had always been kind to me. When he found out, he said he would help me. He said he had a plan…"

His stomach knotted.

"It… it went wrong. Anton brought the wedding day forward…and we were married. Afterwards, he tried to…tried to… And that…that's why I don't like it like that." She stumbled to a halt, with apparent relief, and stared rigidly down at her feet. There was a long silence, but she didn't say any more.

He looked down at her, at the sheen of chestnut hair hiding her face, at the defensive posture, and realised that Holly was not just embarrassed. She was ashamed.

It was Leonie's problem all over again. Being ashamed of something that wasn't her fault.

"Holly?"

"Mmm?"

"Do you blame yourself for what happened?"

Her head jerked up, and for the first time since she'd begun her story, she looked him in the eye. "For the marriage and what came after it I do, yes." Her voice was flat.

"Why?"

"Because I should have planned the escape better. Got away earlier."

"Ah. And Drake should have never gone to the market."

"*What?*"

He saw the moment she got it, read the stunned realisation in her eyes. He reached out to cup her cheek in his hand. "Anton used force against you... The blame and the shame are his, not yours. It wasn't your fault."

"It was." For a second, her expression was acutely vulnerable.

He shook his head. "No, sweetheart. It was *his* fault, all of it. You were a blameless child. Surely you wouldn't blame a thirteen-year-old girl for not being able to defend herself against a grown man?"

"No, of course I wouldn't." She paused, listened to her own words. "No," she said more slowly, "I wouldn't."

"Well then." He stopped. The need to comfort her overrode everything. "Hug?"

Looking somewhat poleaxed, she nodded. He wrapped his arm around her shoulder and dropped a light kiss onto her hair. She felt deceptively small and fragile next to him. He wanted — no, needed — to protect her, and he ached with the knowledge that he could not prevent the evils of the past from hurting her. All he could do was try to make sure that the present and the future were better, and that when the demons haunted her, he was there by her side to support her.

He thought over what she'd told him. "Holly," he said, "you said he tried. What stopped him?"

Shuddering, she said "I fought him. I tried to, anyway. I was losing, but then we were interrupted. The guard, Thomas, came in and said there were police outside. Anton went to deal with them, Thomas grabbed me and managed to get me out."

Thank goodness.

"Then what?"

"Then…I was free."

"What did you do?"

"Oh" — she shrugged — "I lived on the streets for a bit, slept anywhere, survived on what I could find… Having lived in the compound all my life, I had no idea about where to go for help, and I didn't trust anyone, anyway. I was afraid they would send me back."

"Send you back! To a child abuser!"

She grimaced. "I didn't know it was illegal. I had no understanding of the outside world. Fortunately, I discovered libraries, and I spent every day in there reading — partially because it was warm, but also because they had newspapers, books. One of the librarians taught me how to use a computer… That was when I started to write. It was an escape, you see, from the life I was living."

"Yes. I do see."

He swallowed down a wave of nausea. When he thought of all the horrible things that could happen to a young, homeless, defenceless girl, his stomach turned over.

No wonder she supported a charity that helped the homeless. Suddenly, he was fiercely glad he had paid so much for his charity bid. He made a mental note to organise regular donations. And he should talk to the board of trustees. He could probably offer help with finding, refurbishing and maintaining buildings for them.

"Anyway," Holly continued, "eventually, I found 'Help the Homeless' and they rescued me. They helped me sort out a birth certificate. The cult never registered births, and without one, I just didn't exist in the system. It has been lucky in a way, I suppose. It has stopped the press from ever finding out about my past. Anyhow, they sorted out somewhere for me to live, and by that time I was sixteen. I got a job as a cleaner and carried on writing in my spare time and, well, the rest is history."

Chapter Eleven

Like hell. There were a lot of details missing from that account, a lot of horrors left unexplored. But they would come out, in time, and they would deal with them together when they did.

At least she had done it. She had told him the worst. Moving slowly and not wanting to scare her, he wrapped her in his arms. For a moment, she was rigid against him, then all at once she seemed to give in. Pressing her face against his shoulder, she began to cry.

Squeezing his eyes shut, he buried his face against her hair. He loved her so much and could not bear to think of her suffering. He felt like crying himself when he thought of everything she had endured.

A lifetime later, she drew away from him. Guessing that she needed to mop up, he reached inside his bedside drawer and passed her some tissues.

"Thanks." Her voice was muffled, husky. She wiped her eyes, blew her nose.

"Okay, honey?"

"Yes." She folded her arms, still not looking at him. "Sorry for…uh…crying all over you."

"No problem. Feel free to use me as a tissue or a pillow—or anything else, for that matter—whenever you want."

She stiffened. "You… You still want that?"

"What do you mean?"

"After what I told you. After…what he did. You still want me to stay?"

"Holly, what are you talking about?"

"Didn't you hear what I said? He…touched me."

"So?"

"Mac, he *touched* me. Sometimes, I still feel his hands on me. I… I'm…unclean."

"What? You are *not!*" The very idea made him furious. "You think I'd think less of you because some bastard touched you? Think again, Holly."

He looked from her to stare into the shadows in the corner of the room. "I would give everything to be able to turn back the clock and rescue you from him. I hate that it happened. But you? What do I think of *you*? I think you're bloody amazing. You're the strongest woman I've ever met, but I had no idea what kind of fires you'd been through. Does that make me admire you even more? Yes. Does it make me want to shield you from anything that could hurt you ever again? Yes. Does it make me love you even more? *Yes.*"

There was a profound silence. In horror, he realised what he'd done. He'd lost it and he'd told her… everything.

He was screwed.

Why wouldn't I declare undying love after frightening someone half to death whilst making love to them, then forcing them to reveal their deepest trauma?

Way to go, Mac.

Feeling sick, unable even to meet her eyes, he spun away from her.

Outside the window, nothing but fog — thick, dark fog, a swirling expanse of nothingness.

Holly stared at his rigid back in disbelief. What he was saying and doing were so far removed from what she'd expected that she was struggling to reconcile the two.

He was saying he *loved* her? Even after she had told him about Anton?

Warmth washed through her. She had thought that telling him would be the end of everything. But evidently, she had been wrong.

A sudden, euphoric sense of joy swept through her. He *loved* her. He knew everything and he still really loved her.

And she loved him. With sudden certainty, she knew it. All along she had been fighting her attraction, but at every turn she had found herself falling more deeply for him.

She *loved* him. And he had proved himself worthy of that love. Even when confronted by the most sordid of pasts, he hadn't flinched, hadn't backed off, even for a moment. He'd been there for her. As she knew without a shadow of doubt that he always would be.

He was hers. And she was his.

Slowly, she approached him, stopping only when she was in front of him. "You really mean it?" she asked. "Everything you said... That you love me?"

His face hardened. "Yes, why?"

She stroked his cheek and jaw. His early morning stubble was rough against her fingers.

"Show me," she said quietly.

His eyes widened. "Show you?"

She saw it then. Hope where there had been none. She nodded. "Yes. Please. If…you want to."

"If I want to!" A gleam in his eye, relief, joy, sudden determination. Without further ado, he swept her up in his arms. "Right," he said, decisively. "Time for a clean start. I love you, Holly, past and present, body and mind. Every last bit of you. We need to wash off the past and start fresh."

She didn't realise he meant it literally until he had her in the bathroom with her T-shirt and his dressing gown off.

The next moment, they were naked under the warm shower spray and he was kissing her fiercely. Her senses swam and she was gasping for breath. Every memory of Anton was swept away in an instant. There was just here and now, and the two of them, safe and together, loving each other.

He drew back and reached for a bottle of scented bodywash. "Yes?"

"Yes!"

By the time he had stroked and washed every inch of her, she was burning up. After grabbing the bottle, she returned his caresses, quickly becoming distracted as she explored every curve and contour of his strong, lean body. Droplets of water rolled over the hills and valleys of well-defined muscle and clung lovingly to the dark hair on his chest. He was so, so gorgeous. And so, so aroused.

He gave a low groan as she soaped him and he throbbed in her hand. In a gravelly voice, he said, "Turn around. Put your hands on the wall."

What? Shocked, she looked up at him. His eyes were molten, but beneath the blazing passion she thought she saw a quickly hidden glimpse of something else. Nerves. Vulnerability. Disconcerted, she realised that he was not as confident as he seemed.

But why not? He had always been confident with her…until now, until she had doubted him. Had she hurt him when she'd questioned whether he would continue to want her after she'd told him about her past?

With dismay, she realised that she probably had. And now he was testing to see if she did trust him. By asking her to put herself into his hands, in a position where she would be vulnerable…

A surge of protective love had her drawing his head down for a kiss that was hot enough to ignite water. Then, without further ado, she turned and put her hands against the wall. She did trust him, and by the time they got out of this damn shower, he was bloody well going to know it.

He gave a low gasp as she faced the wall and arched her back. The soft spray of the shower ran in warm rivulets down her body. Her long chestnut hair tumbled down her back in damp ringlets.

She glanced over her shoulder and gave him a smile that was pure seduction.

"Holly." He breathed her name like a prayer, then he was drawing her hips towards him and nudging her knees apart with his until she was splayed against him. "Stay there. Right there. Just like that."

He returned a second later, and she realised he'd gone to get a condom. *Just as well.* It hadn't even crossed her mind.

She maintained the stance as he stepped back under the warm shower spray with a murmur of appreciation.

"Don't move," he said and unexpectedly dropped to her knees behind her. Embarrassed, she tried to straighten, but he grabbed her hips. "Please... Please let me."

The yearning in his voice was her undoing. She relaxed, and a second later, his warm tongue lapped against her.

Sensation swirled. All thoughts of embarrassment fled as her pleasure sparked. She squirmed, moaning, gasping as the soft rain of the shower water and the delicate twirl of his tongue combined to build a deep, rolling wave of pleasure.

Her breasts felt full and heavy, and somehow, he must have known, because his soap-slicked hands reached up and around her to play lightly with them. She arched frantically, pressing herself against him, as a sparkle of delight shimmered through her body to her core.

"Mac, please," she gasped as the tension built. "Please, please, please..."

He slid his slippery fingers down, touching her until she was close to exploding, but every time she thought he was going to let her finish, he moved away again until she was all but sobbing his name.

"Mac, *please*..." she pleaded.

"Not yet. Who's touching you?"

"What?" she gasped. "You are!"

"Say my name, Holly."

"Mac. Mac, Mac—"

"Do you feel other hands on you?"

She thought of Anton, his touch, but it was impossible to think of it, to feel it, when Mac's fingers were driving her out of her mind.

"No! I feel you. Only ever you!"

"And are you clean, woman?"

"I—" His hands were on her. His mouth was on her. Water sluiced over her, running down her face like tears. She felt him, alive and vivid all around her, his love and his touch powerful and determined enough to wash away the old taint, and suddenly, for the first time in years, she did feel clean. "Yes," she gasped, "I am—"

Then he circled his long fingers and pressed, and the tension whipped up into a whirling tornado that ripped through her, exploding in a wild, unstoppable, cataclysmic sensation.

As she came down to earth, she sank bonelessly to her knees. As if from a distance, she sensed movement, heard a foil packet being ripped, and Mac knelt behind her, picked her up and settled her onto his knee.

"I'm not done with you yet," he muttered.

Still facing away from him, her knees spread apart by his, she gasped as he slid her straight onto his waiting hardness. Her body, still sensitive, shimmered into life.

"Okay?" he whispered.

"Yes!" Her voice was tight, breathless.

With a low chuckle, he began to move within her. She gasped and her body tightened around him.

He groaned and bit the back of her neck, sending another arc of feeling through her. He licked and nibbled at it, even as he slid his strong hands between her legs to play with her there.

She whimpered. With her legs spread like this, there was no way to control the surges of sensation he was building.

She squirmed desperately as he stroked her, his feather-light touch sending gossamer sensations fluttering through her. Desperate to find some grounding, she grasped his arm, digging her nails in, feeling the iron muscles of his forearm flex. He didn't stop.

She took a sobbing breath, breathing in the mingled scent of soap and aroused man. *Mac.*

She didn't know that she'd cried out his name until he pressed his lips to her shoulder.

"Who's got you, Princess?" he whispered.

Deep inside, he seemed to expand to an impossible hardness.

"You have," she groaned.

"Who'll always have you?"

"You! Please—"

He clamped his other arm around her waist and thrust firmly into her. The heat built, so close...

"And who loves you?"

"You do, you do, *you* do!"

Her voice rose to a scream as he slammed into her. With equal fire she hammered back. He cried out, then wildness overtook them both and they were hurled into a ferocious vortex of unfathomable pleasure.

They were still joined and he was sobbing for breath and shaking violently as he ran possessive hands all over her—breasts, arms, hands, torso, flanks, feet.

"You're mine, Holly," he growled, implacably. "You've got that? And I'm yours, for as long as you want me. And from now on, that's it. You and me together against the world. No matter what comes, whatever you need, I've got you. You understand?"

"Yes."

* * * *

At breakfast, Holly sipped her coffee and watched as Mac cooked sausages and scrambled eggs in nothing but a pair of smooth black boxer shorts and an apron. It was a ridiculous outfit, but on him it just looked hot…insanely hot.

Her insides liquefied as she thought of their time in the shower. He had been so sexy, but at the same time so loving. He had proved to her for once and for all that her past had not repulsed him.

More strangely, his insistent, loving touch had made her feel clean and had somehow erased the ghostly imprint of Anton's hands from years before. Now, she felt so different it was almost like being reborn into a new, unsullied body.

It was wonderful.

She knew she ought to feel a bit freaked out by the possessiveness Mac had shown in the shower. 'You're mine,' he'd said, and once upon a time that would have terrified her. But he'd countered that with, 'And I'm yours,' and she'd understood that Mac's brand of possessiveness was just protective, not oppressive. It had, in an odd way, made her feel warm and wanted. And she couldn't deny that she felt like that about him too. He was hers and she'd protect him to her dying breath.

And that thought pulled her up short. She really would do that. Her love for him was that strong.

Worried, she thought about it. Did her feelings mean she was becoming like her mother? Was she going to turn into someone soft and sappy, made helpless by love? Was she going to end up dependent on him for her happiness? She knew she was changing. Was she going to lose herself, her independence, her emotional freedom?

Taking a gulp of coffee, she promised herself that she wouldn't allow that to happen. She would not allow her identity to be subsumed until she was nothing but a cipher. She would not be a slave to love.

I will not *be like my mother.*

Mac set a plate down before her, then sat opposite with his own breakfast. With a nod of thanks, she began to eat.

"Mmm. This is good," she murmured.

He glanced at her and grinned. "That's because you asked for scrambled eggs. I'm absolutely terrible at fried eggs."

She laughed. "Well, I'm terrible at cooking, full-stop, so I'll be appreciative, no matter what you make."

They tucked in, relaxed in each other's company. Holly couldn't help but imagine Drake and Isabella in a similar situation. Would they, too, sit and share a meal in harmony in the end?

A lot needed to be resolved between them before that could happen. As a victim of kidnapping, Drake might feel like she had after being trapped in the commune—besmirched and doubtful that anyone could really love him. Isabella would have to address those issues. Would she do it head-on, as Mac had done, demanding that Drake acknowledge her love, her touch? Would she fight to make him feel clean, as Mac had done for her? Not just physically but spiritually? Maybe, once Isabella and the slaves had rescued Drake, they should take the traumatised man to a sanctuary—a monastery, an abbey…somewhere where emotional and physical healing could take place. There, Isabella could fight for Drake, heal him with her love.

"More coffee?" She came back into the present to find Mac watching her wryly.

"Uh, yes, please."

He turned to the percolator. "You looked a long way away just then. Thinking about your book?"

She flushed. "Sorry, yes. Occupational hazard."

He smiled easily. "You want to do some writing today? Or Monopoly, perhaps?"

"Maybe. What are you going to do?"

Mac looked at her thoughtfully. "Oh, I've got loads to do," he said. "To tell you the truth, I've been making some changes."

"Oh, yes?"

"Mm." He set the mugs down in front of them. "Yes. I thought a lot about what you said when we had lunch in London that day. You asked me if I was fulfilled by my job. And I told you that, apart from the designing element of my work, I wasn't."

"I remember."

"Well, I decided to do something about it. I've got a backlog of work from when Leonie was kidnapped, but once that's done, I'm restructuring the business. I've promoted some of my oldest, most loyal employees – some who even worked for my parents before me – to more senior roles. They're very capable, and it's a way of rewarding and thanking them. They are going to take over the running of the business, and I'm just going to concentrate on the design side."

"Oh! That's excellent!"

He grinned. "It feels great. I realised that I'd made enough money to last me and Leonie a lifetime – probably our children's lifetimes, too. So why was I driving myself so hard and using up my life doing things I didn't care about? From now on, I'll be focusing on what I do best—and spending more time with my friends and family. In the future, I want to enjoy my time with the people I love most."

He looked at her steadily, and she had an uneasy feeling that he was including her in that statement.

With a nod, she said, "That sounds good," and hoped she'd misread the flicker of disappointment she'd seen in his eyes.

She stood up abruptly. This was too much. She was getting too drawn in. She *couldn't* give herself up to love like this. "I... I need to go and write," she said, abruptly.

"Okay." His voice was steady and understanding. "I'll see you later."

* * * *

Later that afternoon, Mac and Holly were sat in the kitchen having a tea break when Mac received a call.

"Mac, it's James."

"Oh, hi. How's London?"

There was a pause. Then James said fervently, "Absolutely excellent," before clearing his throat. "That's not why I'm ringing you, though. We're just outside of Edinburgh at the moment. There've been some developments in Holly's case. Mac, I've found out a bit about Holly's past—"

Conscious of Holly on the stool opposite, Mac said, "Mmm, so have I."

"Does she know I'm helping with the case?"

"Ah...no."

"Okay. I need to tell her. You'd better put her on loudspeaker for this."

Mac glanced at Holly then said, "It's James. He wants me to put him on speaker."

Looking a little startled, Holly nodded. "Okay."

James' voice came through clearly. "Hi, Holly," he said.

"Hi, James. What's up?"

There was a pause, then James said, "Holly, I've got a confession to make."

"Oh, yes?"

"Yes. When I heard you had a stalker, I offered Liberty's services to the police. I wanted to do it to thank you for helping Leonie—and because we're friends, of course—but I thought I'd only tell you if we had any success. Not much use otherwise."

"Oh! Well, thank you. But...you are telling me. You've had a breakthrough?"

"Yes. I don't think you're going to like it, though. Holly, I'm sorry, but I we've traced the stalker... It's Anton Devereaux."

"*What?*"

Holly was off her stool and backing away from the phone as if it were a poisonous snake before he'd finished speaking.

After dropping the phone on the counter, Mac caught her up in his arms, holding her shivering body tight. "I've got you, Holly," he whispered.

"The police also think he's been running drugs and guns. They've surrounded the compound but... Wait! Shots have been fired. Hold on..." There was a pause. Mac heard Leonie's staccato voice in the background. "Leonie says to put the news on. It's on now..."

Grabbing the remote control, Mac switched on the kitchen TV. Immediately, footage could be seen from helicopters circling the compound. Armed police surrounded the place. Random shots were being fired. A newsreader was reporting that an anonymous woman had tipped off the police about the activities of the cult and its leader.

Holly bit her knuckles. "My mother's in there," she breathed.

"James...you and Leonie are there?" asked Mac.

"Yes. We've just arrived. The stalker investigation only intersected with the gun and drug case at the last minute. If I'd been here sooner, I might have been able to prevent this mess."

"Okay." Mac looked down at the distraught woman in his arms. "You want to go?" he asked quietly.

"What? Yes!"

"Right. We're on our way now. Where are you staying?"

"Nowhere. Haven't had time —" Shots sounded in the background. James sounded tense. "Listen... I've got to go."

"Okay, I'll sort out the arrangements. We'll meet you there."

"Right."

The call ended. Holly stepped out of his arms and ran a shaky hand through her hair. Disbelievingly, she said, "Anton. Bloody Anton. I never even thought about it being him. I knew he was a vengeful person, but it's been years since I got away..."

Deep inside, Mac felt an uncontrollable rage coiling. This man had been the bane of Holly's life and had got away with it for far too long. No matter what happened tonight, he vowed to himself that he was going to make sure this guy was dealt with...whatever it took.

"And my mother... What if something happens to her?"

Mac's jaw clenched. "It won't," he said. "I'll call for a helicopter now. Can you throw some clothes into a bag?"

Chapter Twelve

Three hours later, as darkness fell, they flew over the Firth of Forth. The arches of the Forth Bridge were lit up with gleaming gold lights, reflecting off the dark water, whilst in the distance, Edinburgh Castle towered over the ancient capital of Scotland.

Holly looked down over the familiar landmarks and knew that, by helicopter, they were only minutes away.

She clenched Mac's hand. He'd been solicitous but largely silent throughout the flight, only occasionally interrupting her fragmented thoughts to tell her about arrangements he'd made or to ask if she wanted something to drink or a bite to eat. But there was no way she could eat at the moment. She was too upset and too worried about her mother.

That intense anxiety surprised her. She'd long thought that any affection for her mother was gone. When her mother had supported her marriage to Anton, it had been the last straw for her. She had realised that Anton meant far more to her mother than she did, and that betrayal had cut deep.

But it seemed as if she'd been lying to herself. Faced with the prospect of harm coming to her mother, she discovered that she did care, very much indeed. She was just praying that her mother was alive and safe so that she could see her and talk to her again.

Her reverie was interrupted by the pilot's announcement that they were preparing to land. Mac had already told her that a car would be waiting to take them straight to the compound, and she couldn't help but be grateful for his reassuring support. His powerful presence was an enormous help in the circumstances.

Biting her lip, she cautioned herself not to become too reliant on the wonderful man beside her. It would be so easy to take the solace he so freely offered, to seek comfort in his arms, to lean on him to see her through the horrors of this event. But that was the path to dependency. If she gave in to that need, she would be no better than her mother. No, she needed to stand on her own two feet, no matter what.

"We're here." Mac's voice in her headphones was steady as they started to descend. "We're only ten minutes away from the compound by car. There's been another message from James. The police are getting ready to take the place by force."

Holly wouldn't have wished the car journey that followed on her worst enemy. The country roads outside of Edinburgh were narrow and winding. The driver did his best to navigate them quickly, appreciating the urgency. Holly was momentarily and queasily reminded of Harry Potter's journey on the Knight Bus.

But mercifully they soon arrived, slewing to a halt behind a phalanx of police cars. In the distance, shots were being fired. James and Leonie were waiting for them as they got out.

"There's been a breakthrough," James said, dispensing with usual greetings. "We've had another call from the woman who gave us the original tip-off about the guns and drugs. She says she's in the compound. Her name is Tabitha."

"Tabitha?" Holly's face tightened. "That's my mother."

"Yes." James was unsurprised and she realised that he must have done his research and already known about her mother—and her upbringing. A wave of embarrassed shame washed over her. Mac stretched a warm arm around her shoulder to pull her into his side at the same moment that James broke off and said sharply, "Holly, stop it! None of this is on you. You've nothing—not one thing in the world—to feel ashamed about. You were just a kid, unlucky enough to be caught up in a terrible situation."

Leonie stepped forward, her face serious. "Yes, Holly. You taught me that lesson. Now it's time to take your own advice. None of this was—or is—your fault. And no matter what, we have your back, Holly. We're your family now. Whatever happens here today, we're with you."

Holly felt Leonie's words like a punch in the gut. She tried to take a step back but was prevented by Mac's firm hold on her.

What were they doing to her? How could she stay independent and stand alone, when they were so intent on gathering round her, helping her? How could she resist the lure of such care, such affection, the impossible promise of belonging to a family, something she'd never had?

Feeling pressured, she said, "I can't do this… I don't know anything about being in a family."

Mac's grip on her shoulder tightened. James stepped forward and took her hand in his. "There are many different kinds of families," James said quietly. "And this one—me, Mac, Leonie—we are yours. You don't have to *do* anything. There's no obligation. You're not trapped by us, but we're here for you."

Oh, hell. She could feel herself sliding into the trap of loving them all, of wanting to belong, to have people of her own. But deep inside, she still felt scared. Her mother had been her family but had put Anton before her, betraying her trust. What if she opened herself up again, believed in them, and they let her down? She'd never be able to cope with it.

She watched a pulse throb in James' jaw and realised he had more to say. She had never seen him look so hard, so intent. His guise of ordinariness had been shed. The tough man beneath was visible. His stare pierced hers. "But, Holly, I have something to tell you that may shock you." He paused then said, "Holly, your mother told the police that she had called them because she had discovered Anton was harassing you, and she was afraid he would go further and try to kill you."

"What?" There was no way. Holly shook her head. "But that's impossible. My mother would never do that. She was totally besotted with him—"

James shook his head. "That may have been true in the past, but it doesn't appear to be so now. She gave the police enough information to bring him down and put him away for years. She was taking one hell of a risk to contact them. If Anton had caught her…"

He would have killed her. Holly knew that for a fact and was sure her mother knew it, too. Her mother had risked her life for *her*?

Something deep inside fractured painfully. Her mother *did* care for her. She had put her before Anton. It was a miracle. Tears were welling and Holly forced them back.

But she couldn't break down like this. She needed backbone. She needed to *cope* as she always had in the past. Gathering her thoughts, she asked "So, what's happening now?"

James expelled a harsh breath. "Now, they have a problem. Your mother said she and about twenty other people are being held hostage in a locked room at the back of the compound. A man put there to guard them — Thomas — is trying to break them out. They're worried that Anton and his men might set fire to the compound and try to kill them all. It sounds as if they've realised how dangerous and insane he is."

Holly drew in a sharp breath and sweat prickled down her back as she tried to control her desperate reaction to the thought of her mother and a room full of other people being trapped in a burning building. But, she thought, clutching at straws, at least Thomas was there — big, strong, dependable Thomas, who had once risked everything to help her escape. He would be doing everything, she knew, to get them out. But it might not be enough. "We have to do something," she whispered. "Anton would sooner kill them than let them go."

James nodded. "I agree. They're trying to keep him and his men pinned down by gunfire at the front of the building. There are officers at the back, attempting to get in. They can't use a battering ram or explosives because they don't want Anton to know what's happening. They're worried that if he finds out, he'll shoot them all."

For a moment, black spots danced in front of Holly's eyes. She wasn't an idiot. She'd read about cults and sieges in the past, and she knew how badly things could go. But the thought of her mother and Thomas being caught up in such a situation made her feel lightheaded and nauseous.

Mac must have felt her reaction, because a second later she found herself wrapped in his strong arms. "Easy, sweetheart," he said gruffly. "One step at a time."

James' radio crackled into life. He spoke into it briefly. "Thomas managed to break the door down and open the back exit. The police are getting them out now, then they're going after Anton. I need to go."

Holly's head jerked up. "Where…where are you going?" Her eyes fell on Leonie, who looked pale and tense.

James' gaze softened. "I'm a negotiator, Holly," he said, quietly. "This is what I do. I have to get Anton and his people to come out peacefully if I can."

Holly stared at him and swallowed. Suddenly the reality of his job hit home. "You can't," she said, dryly. "He's not rational. He thinks he's a god. You won't be able to reason with him."

"I hear you, Holly," he said, grimly. "And what you've told me will guide me in what to say to him. But I have to do it. I have to try."

He turned to Leonie and took her in his arms. "Leonie…my Leonie…" He pressed a kiss to her hair. "I love you," he whispered—and he was gone.

For the next fifteen minutes, she huddled with them, helpless to do anything but watch and wait. In the shadows, James, armed and dressed in a bullet-proof jacket, moved with a team of police towards the compound.

They vanished into the darkness and Leonie gave a dry sob. Mac must have heard it too, because in the next moment, all three of them were holding onto each other.

"Have faith, Leonie," Mac whispered. "James is experienced at this — and he's good at it."

Abruptly, Holly realised that Mac had already endured a similar agony in his past. He must have had a similar torturous wait for news of Leonie's rescue. Suddenly, she understood how much it must be costing him to be there. She wrapped her arms more tightly around him. "I've got you, Mac," she whispered, and a shudder ran through him.

In the next moment, all hell seemed to break loose. From inside the compound there were shouts and a thundering volley of shots. Lightning flashes lit up the darkness and dark figures ran from the compound. All was chaos.

For a minute, they searched the scene, trying in vain to see what was happening, desperate for a glimpse of James, then a black-clad figure was sprinting towards them.

"James," Leonie breathed, and she was running to meet him. He lifted her to spin her round, then he was kissing her with a hunger that was unmistakable, even in the dark from a distance.

Holly glanced up at Mac and he was smiling. "You knew?" she asked. "And you don't mind?"

"Yes," he said, "and no. Did you see it coming?"

Holly couldn't help but laugh. "I saw James persuade Leonie to go to London. I thought then that there was something going on between them."

He looked at her wryly. "I didn't think they'd get it past you," he said.

At that moment, James and Leonie appeared, breathless and rumpled. Leonie looked flustered, whilst James grinned at them ruefully.

"Right," he said. "Ah…sorry about that." He cleared his throat. "Well, Anton opened fire on us and got himself shot, the stupid sod. He's alive—for now at least—and on his way to the hospital. Not sure he'll make it, though. The hostages are safe. They're in a hospital tent being triaged before being taken to the hospital. Holly, do you want to see your mother?"

Holly froze. Did she? All these years, she'd bitterly resented her mother for choosing Anton over her. Now it appeared that things had changed, and she'd finally put her daughter first. But was it too little, too late?

But then she thought about how she'd felt when she'd learned her mother's life was at risk. She'd been desperate to see her. And she realised that time was too short to let old resentments stand in the way. Nodding, she took a firm hold of Mac's hand and, with considerable trepidation, went to face her mother.

The tent was chaotic. Doctors and nurses were checking people over, while ambulances waited outside.

James spoke briefly to a policewoman who pointed them to the far corner. And there on a bench was Thomas, with his arm around her mother.

"Mum," Holly whispered. "Oh, mum." And she was running towards her mother and they were in each other's arms, crying.

Finally, they pulled apart. "Holly, my baby," Tabitha breathed. "You're okay. You're alive, and you're all grown up…"

Holly gave her a wobbly smile. If she had grown, her mother had aged. Streaks of grey ran through her mother's once-chestnut hair and there were lines around her eyes and mouth. But she was still as beautiful as ever.

"Yes," she said. "Mum, are you and Thomas all right? You're not hurt?"

Her mother shook her head. "No, love, we're fine."

Thomas stepped forward and hesitated. For a moment, Holly wondered why, until she recalled the last time they'd seen each other, when he'd rescued her from Anton's bed. Then she had been traumatised, battered and bruised after trying to fight off Anton. She had a sudden memory of his tears when he'd found her. Stepping forward, she deliberately wrapped her arms around him and gave him a firm hug. She wasn't a scared teenager anymore. He exhaled, his big body relaxed and she was enveloped in his strong arms. In a gruff voice, he said roughly, "I'm glad you're all right, lass."

She stepped back. "I am," she said, quietly. "Thomas…there was no time to say it then, but thank you for rescuing me."

A sudden frown marred his brow. "Thank…me?" He paused. "Holly, we need to talk. But first, perhaps, you'd better introduce us to your friends."

* * * *

Two hours later, they sat in an elegant private lounge in The Prism, a renowned hotel in Edinburgh designed and part-owned by Mac.

Things had happened at breakneck speed since Anton had been apprehended. Wasting no time, Mac had liaised with the authorities, cutting through red tape like a hot knife through butter. As a result, suites had been arranged for her and Mac, her mother and Thomas and James and Leonie. In addition, hotel rooms had been booked and transport arranged for all the hostages who were well enough to leave the hospital. Despite the late hour, personal shoppers were providing clothes and toiletries for everyone. The dining room had been opened and chefs retained to provide meals throughout the night. Holly had tried to thank Mac, but he had shaken his head. "It's only right," he said quietly. "These people have been through an ordeal. They need our support."

In that moment, Holly understood just how deeply she loved him. How could she not? He had all the power of an alpha male, but he was driven by his protective instincts and the will to use his resources for good. He *cared* about people—even people he didn't know. He had a conscience, morals and was motivated by kindness. And he loved her.

It was wonderful and terrifying all at the same time.

She held on to the thought of his love and support, and that of James and Leonie, as she settled herself on a sumptuous sofa with Mac by her side. She had a feeling that the conversation she was about to have with her mother was going to be a difficult one.

They waited until drinks had been served before Thomas said tentatively, "Holly, earlier you thanked me for rescuing you."

"Yes."

"Well, there are things that you don't know about that time. Things we need to tell you."

Holly watched in disbelief as Thomas reached over to hold her mother's clenched hand. *Are they a couple?*

Tabitha took a deep breath. "Yes. First of all, I have to say I'm so sorry—sorry for ever joining Anton's group, sorry for the way you grew up. We were just kids when we joined, but we should have known better. By the time we did, we couldn't get out."

Confused, Holly asked, "We?"

"Me and your mother, Holly. We were...are...a couple. But you know Anton didn't allow people to pair off, so we kept it a secret. But we've always loved each other. Always."

Holly looked at them in disbelief. "Am I... Am I..." She was frightened to ask, terrified of the answer. *Am I Anton's daughter?*

Thomas' face softened. "You're ours, Holly," he said, gently.

A torrent of memories ran through her head at his words—Thomas telling her stories, carving toys out of wood, teaching her to read, to write—and risking everything to get her out of the compound...

Relief rushed through her. Thomas was her father. Kind, decent, brave Thomas, not Anton. She took a swift gulp of her wine. "Oh, Thomas," she breathed, "I'm so glad it's you..."

His face contorted. "I'm sorry," he said gruffly. "So sorry we exposed you to that lunatic. When your mother told me that he planned to marry you, we couldn't believe it. He'd known you since you were a baby." The revulsion in his tone was evident. "We knew we had to find a way to get you out. We made a plan, but when he brought the date of your marriage forward, it was a nightmare."

Across the table, Leonie gasped. "Holly, you're *married*?"

Holly clenched her fists. She shook her head. "No. It wasn't a legal marriage. I was only thirteen."

She glimpsed a muscle throb in James' jaw in her peripheral vision. Leonie winced. "Oh, no. Holly, I'm so sorry."

"Luckily, I got out before the marriage was consummated." A thought occurred to her. "But, Thomas…you said you made a plan together? With mum? That's not right. Mum said it would be an honour for me to marry him."

At the accusing anger in Holly's voice, Tabitha's eyes filled with tears. "Oh, my darling girl. I'm so sorry. I had to say that. We couldn't let anyone know we opposed the marriage. If anyone had suspected us, we'd have been watched like hawks, and we'd never have got you out. In our original plan, we hoped to escape with you, but as it was, there was no time. We just had to grab you and get you away. There was no opportunity to explain anything. And after you'd gone, Anton clamped down so much there was no way to get out." She wiped tears away. "All these years, we've worried so much about you being out in the world, unprotected…and I was terrified that we might never get the chance to see you again to explain the truth — that we loved you and wanted to protect you."

Holly stared at her. "But you loved Anton! You were on his side —"

Tabitha shook her head firmly. "No. I haven't been on his side for many years. But I couldn't show my opposition. You know what he did to anyone who disagreed with him. I was frightened he might take it out on you if I did. So, I pretended…"

Holly felt sick. She had been so wrong about her mother. Far from being the simpering, devoted sap she had thought her, her mother had actually been secretly opposing Anton all these years, and had, in fact, risked her life twice — once to liberate her and again tonight to get everyone else out.

Holly looked at her mother, finally seeing the strength and the courage of the woman before her. "Oh, mum," she said, huskily, "I —"

At that moment, James' mobile buzzed. He picked it up, glanced at the screen and his face darkened. Clearing his throat, he said quietly, "Holly, I'm sorry to interrupt, but that was the police. They wanted to let us know that Anton died ten minutes ago."

Chapter Thirteen

Mac eyed Holly warily. She was prowling round the hotel suite giving an excellent impression of a caged tiger.

The party had broken up soon after James' bombshell announcement. It had been one stress too many on top of an awful day. So now they were back upstairs, and it was evident that something – and there were so many things to choose from – had seriously upset Holly.

With a vicious flick of her foot, she kicked off first one high heel then the other before stalking across to the huge panoramic glass sliding doors that framed a glorious view of the city.

With a huff of annoyance, she slid them open and stepped out onto the balcony, into the cool night air and the sounds of the city.

The lights glinted off her glowing chestnut hair, the shadows fell across her face and the whip-sharp tension she was holding in her slim body was apparent as she folded her arms.

Something wrenched inside him at the sight. She was so self-sufficient, but he wanted the arms around her to be his, to ease her when she was suffering.

Not that he thought she'd let him touch her at the moment. No, she was too stressed for that.

But he needed to find a way to help her relax. Until he did, there was no way he was going to get her to tell him what exactly was wrong.

He poured two brandies, switched off the lights so the room was bathed only in soft moonlit shadows and the glow of the city, and went out onto the balcony.

"Beautiful night," he said. It was. The stars were clear and bright in a crisp night sky and there was a full moon.

She took an incautious swig of her drink and coughed. "Yeah."

She wasn't even seeing it. Mac could see that all her attention was taken up by whatever was going on in that quick, clever brain of hers.

"Want to talk about it?" he said mildly.

She swung round to face him, her face hard and full of tension. "No," she said, "I think I want to go to bed."

He rocked back on his heels. He hadn't been expecting that. "All right, then," he said.

To his consternation, she threw back the rest of her brandy recklessly.

"Holly—" he said uneasily, but she shook her head so hard that her beautiful hair fanned out in an arc around her. His body reacted. She was so beautiful.

"No," she said, "no words." After grabbing him by the hand, she hauled him into the bedroom.

She was like a force of nature then, divesting both of them of their clothes in record time before tumbling them both onto the bed. He'd thought he would be gentle with her, comfort her after the ravages of the day, but she wanted none of that. She was full of fire and fury, and he realised that he'd been wrong in his assessment of how she was feeling. She was not upset or distressed. She was *angry*.

She was full of hell and brimming with rage, and he had a sudden sense that she was showing him, telling him, about feelings she couldn't put into words.

She savaged his mouth with hers and his control shattered. Raw passion burned inside him, and he kissed her, giving no quarter, holding nothing back. Her nails raked over his shoulders and the sting spurred him on. He ran his hands roughly down her body, feeling every gorgeous curve and precious valley, and swore to himself that he would protect her with his life for the rest of his days.

She bit his neck, and lightning arced through him. With a roar, he wrapped his arms round her and rolled her on top of him. Without warning, she reared up and slammed herself down on him. *Hell.* He arched violently, grabbing her hips to hold her there.

She clutched his shoulders. "I'm so damn furious," she ground out, pounding down on him. Pleasure sank its fangs into him as her heat wrapped around him.

She rose above him like an avenging angel. Her breasts were beautiful in the moonlight.

"I'm so *furious*. All these years, I was frightened to love."

She slammed down again. He gasped —

"Frightened that if I did, I would turn into a simpering, vulnerable, weak woman like my mother."

His body hardened into a pulsing throb. It almost hurt. *Wait! What?* She'd been frightened to *love*?

"And all this time, it was a lie. She wasn't like that at all. She was *fighting*!"

He was fighting too, fighting for control. He needed to hold on. She was telling him things, telling him the *truth*. Was this why she'd been holding back from him?

"I thought that love just left you open to betrayal, like she betrayed me."

Grief and love and sudden understanding rolled through him, even as his body screamed for release.

"But she didn't. She *did* love me."

She suddenly lifted off him, leaving him gasping for breath, his body reaching for release.

Bending down, she kissed him passionately. He melted at the feel of her warm lips on his, the stroke of her long hair against his cheeks, his neck. She looked down into his eyes. "Well, no more," she whispered roughly. "I'll not let my childhood, not let Anton, wreck my life in any way ever again."

Holding onto his shoulders, she rolled onto her back, pulling him over her. He stiffened. She didn't like it like that. For a moment, he resisted her, but she shook her head. "No," she whispered, "I love you, Mac. I love you and I trust you. Make love to me like this."

His heart jumped. She *loved* him. She loved him, and she'd told him. *Finally.* Incandescent joy ran through him, swiftly doused by sudden, sharp anxiety. What she was asking was terrifying. What if he frightened her?

"You're sure?" he whispered hoarsely. "You don't have to do this."

"Yes. Yes, I do. We do. We have to defeat Anton."

He stared at her, seeing the need and the vulnerability in her eyes. The sight infuriated him. He'd sworn earlier that day to deal with Anton once and for all. He hadn't imagined it would be like this.

But he would do it. He would wipe Anton's legacy of pain and fear away if it was the last thing he did.

Tenderly, he stroked a stray strand of hair away from her face. "I love you, Princess," he said deeply. "You're safe. But we don't have to win this fight today. If you need to stop, you tell me. Yes?"

"Yes."

He kissed her then, telling her without words how much he loved her.

He readied himself. Every instinct said he needed to do this quickly, before she had time to panic.

He nudged against her. She gasped into his mouth and he took advantage of her involuntary reaction to deepen the kiss. At the same moment, he slid into her.

He raised his head and saw her eyes dilate. He froze, fighting the irresistible urge to thrust. She felt so wonderful—

Then she grabbed his shoulders, pulling him down for another kiss as she bucked her hips up to meet his.

He just had time to groan out, "Don't close your eyes," before he was swept under, engulfed in a wave of wild pleasure so intense that it robbed him of the power to think, to speak, to do anything except *feel*.

Beneath him she went crazy, not fighting him but fighting *with* him, surging up against him. He looked into her eyes, grabbing her gaze with his and holding it.

The tide of pleasure rose, and sensations built. There was not a hint, not a single thought of Anton tainting their lovemaking. He laughed out loud, triumphant, full of joy, and she looked up at him. Understanding flashed across her face. She was laughing too, then everything grew too intense, laughing was forgotten, feelings swirled and coalesced, and suddenly they were there, together, spinning off into the sun.

Afterwards, when he came to his senses, he pulled her into his arms, burying his face in her hair. "You all right, Holly?"

She cuddled into him. "Oh, yes," she said, sleepily, "perfect."

He watched as her eyelids fluttered shut and her breathing slowed, then he pressed fervent lips to her forehead. "Yes, sweetheart," he whispered huskily, "yes. You really are."

Chapter Fourteen

When she woke the next morning, he wasn't there.

She was disconcerted for a moment, then the door opened and he came in, looking surprised to see her awake.

"Hi," he said, kissing her gently. "I thought you'd be asleep. It's not dawn yet."

"Why are *you* awake?"

He smiled and shrugged. "Oh, you know," he said, "places to go, people to see."

"In the middle of the night?"

He grinned. "Not quite. Still, since you're awake, do you fancy going for a walk? We could watch the sun rise."

She looked into his warm blue eyes and felt a surge of love. Last night she'd told him she loved him. She could hardly believe it. "Okay," she said, sitting up, "fifteen minutes and you're on!"

To her surprise, there was a car waiting when they went downstairs. Mac bundled her in and they set off.

"Where are we going?" she asked. The city streets were deserted, save for an occasional tram. "I thought we were going for a walk?"

"We are. Patience, sweetheart."

Finally, the car stopped, and they got out. Mac dropped a mischievous kiss on her nose and took her hand.

"Where are we?" she asked, looking around, mystified. Before her was a stone wall and a grassy slope.

"You've never been here before?"

"No."

He smiled. "Come on. I'll show you."

They walked up the slope as the sun rose. A soft breeze brushed through the grass. Birds sang in joyful profusion—chaffinches and warblers, sparrows and thrushes—the dawn chorus, celebrating the new day. The morning sun tinted the sky with pink and gold as they walked.

Reaching the summit, Holly came to a sudden, startled halt. The whole of Edinburgh lay before her, beautiful in the early morning light. The castle, the steeples of churches, the ribbons of road and rows of houses stretched out to distant misty mountains.

She turned in a full circle, taking in the city and the shimmering loch in the distance. Everything was rose-coloured, pink-washed, magical.

She turned and found Mac watching her, a curiously intense expression on his face. "Mac, this is Arthur's Seat! I've always wanted to come here!"

He laughed. "It's one of my favourite places. I thought you might like it."

"Oh, it's beautiful…perfect."

She grinned as she suddenly realised that she would have to bring Drake and Isabella here. After everything, after Isabella had healed Drake, she would bring him here to this soul-restoring view...

He touched her cheek with his warm fingers. "Last night, you said you were afraid to love, to become as vulnerable as you thought your mother was. Do you still feel that way?"

She flushed, caught hold of the gentle hand against her cheek with her own. "No," she said, softly. "Last night, I realised I can love and still be strong...still be myself."

He gave a crooked grin. "I was hoping you'd say that," he said. "I love who you really are." He suddenly dropped to one knee on the soft grass. Holly's heart stopped, then beat again in double-quick time.

Reaching inside his jacket, he took out a ring box. Flipping it open, he revealed a beautiful ring, a ruby edged with sparkling diamonds.

She gasped. "Oh! It's beautiful!"

"It was my mother's. I got them to fly it up from the island this morning. If you don't like it, we can get you something different —"

"No! This one is lovely...special."

His eyes softened. "Like you," he said. "Holly Mason, I know I don't deserve you, but I do love you...always and forever, come what may. Sweetheart, I dare you... Will you marry me?"

* * * *

They were married a month later in the tiny stone chapel on the edge of Old Town Bay on St. Mary's.

It was a sparklingly sunny day. Sunlight glittered off the sea, seagulls wheeled and the air was fragrant with the scent of flowers.

Holly was wearing a beautiful ivory silk wedding gown. She'd chosen it because it was gorgeous, and the faintly eighteenth-century styling reminded her of Isabella.

She was feeling an enormous sense of satisfaction. She'd sworn to herself that she would finish the book before the wedding — and she'd just made it. Drake and Isabella were now married. In the future, their adventures would be as a couple. To her satisfaction, the character based on James was getting on very well with the one based on Leonie, too, and she rather thought that another marriage might be in the offing in the next book.

It certainly was in real life. Leonie, who along with Melissa was acting as her bridesmaid, was now sporting a beautiful diamond engagement ring. The trip to London had been eventful in more ways than one. Now, she and James were inseparable and clearly bursting with happiness.

Her father walked her down the aisle while her mother stood nearby, clutching a damp hanky. The couple were delighting in their newfound freedom. Mac had bought them a house on St. Mary's. They had decided they wanted to be close to their daughter. And they had both found work — her mother as a cook and her father as a gardener. It was clear they were loving life on the beautiful island.

But for now, there was just the quiet, ancient stone church with sunlight flooding through the stained-glass window, dappling the floor with colour. There was the scent of yellow roses, chosen to represent freedom. There was Mac, waiting at the altar for her, his face aglow with love and happiness. And as the organ finished playing, as Thomas gave her to Mac and as she placed her hand in his, she knew she that today was just the beginning and that whatever the future held, they would face it together, hand in hand...in love.

Want to see more like this?
Here's a taster for you to enjoy!

Anywhere and Always:
Falling for the Tycoon
Aurora Russell

Excerpt

The sky was a perfect unending blue, clear and brilliant, its beauty rivaled only by the magnificent expanse of bright aqua ocean and baby-powder-fine sand. It had always been Annelise's dream to see the Caribbean, and she knew she should have been happy. Ecstatic. Wasn't she still here, even if she was alone? But, instead, she just felt empty. Detached.

She'd cried her tears. So many tears. For weeks. Wondering what had gone wrong to make Kyle decide to walk out on their life together, ending their wedding and honeymoon plans abruptly. Wondering what would come next. Looking at the space where his toothbrush used to sit next to the bathroom sink, looking at the empty space in the fridge where the special espresso he loved had always been kept, she'd felt a gnawing, painful ache in her chest, raw like a sucking wound. She'd sobbed into her pillow, worried she'd alarm the neighbors in the condo above. Her hot tears signaled the end of not just a seven-year-long relationship, but also of her dreams for the future. She'd cried so much she'd gone numb.

She'd managed the chores of daily living — making food, getting dressed, going to work and to the store — but she'd felt like an imposter, like some zombie trapped inside the body of the vivacious, happy, hopeful woman she'd always been. She'd looked in the mirror and it had scared her. But still, nothing moved her anymore — not sadness, not anger, not understanding or judgment. Nothing. When the reminder from the travel agency had come through as an alert on her smartphone, the hot swell of anger had been as surprising as it had been fleeting. That spark was what had led her to do the crazy thing she'd done. Just to feel something, anything, she'd decided to take their honeymoon. Alone.

Logically, the decision had been clear. She should go — two weeks in a remote section of the Yucatan Peninsula, staying at an exclusive hotel right on the beach. It was a two-hour-long ride in a Jeep on bumpy roads through the jungle to get to the collection of luxury cabanas, perched right at the edge of a wild natural preserve. Quite a journey, but it was supposed to be worth it. This was her dream trip, and it was almost entirely paid for already…and non-refundable. When they'd booked it, she hadn't even had a nanosecond of concern about that portion of the terms and conditions. The idea that Kyle would have chosen not to go would have been laughable to her on that long-ago morning. After seven years of blissful love, she'd thought she'd known him inside and out. She had never been more wrong.

The decision to come had been more complex. Could she handle the possible emotional roller-coaster of going on what was supposed to be the romantic trip of a lifetime by herself? Was she crazy to risk putting herself through a possible ordeal of 'what-ifs' and 'might-have-beens'? But when she'd looked down at that small phone screen, slightly smudged from her fingers, and had again seen the hollow, eerie eyes in her dark reflection, she'd known. She was going to go. Her best friend, Marina, was the only one who seemed to understand and support her decision. Everyone else just looked at her like she'd lost her mind.

She hadn't been able to muster much enthusiasm for the packing, but still, even just knowing that she was packing to go had made her feel a little less frozen. Instead of staring at the same walls where she'd hung pictures with Kyle, or sitting on the same couch they'd spent several happy hours picking out at the furniture store, she would escape — or so she'd thought. But of course, she couldn't ever escape. Not really. She couldn't run away from herself.

So here she stood, looking at the prettiest view she'd ever seen, hands-down. The warm breeze ruffled her hair and the air held the delicate scent of tropical flowers mixed with the tangy salt of the ocean. Even the sound of the waves lapping onto the soft sand was exquisite. Soothing. And she could appreciate it all, but only in the abstract. Here in paradise, she was still frozen. Annelise sighed and turned, determined to keep walking until she began to thaw, even if it was just a little. Maybe seeing the jungle would help. She'd read there were even toucans. She sighed again, more heavily this time, trying to feel a glimmer of her usual optimism. Marina's voice replayed in her head, encouraging her. And with Marina's own past sadness, her advice meant even more.

'Go on, girl,' her friend had said. *'Don't let that man take one more day of your life. You have too much in you left to give. Go wild! Do anything and everything because you never know what's around the corner.'*

With those words in mind, Annelise doggedly continued, sinking her heels into the softer sand farther away from the waterline. It truly was incredible to be alone in such an unbelievably beautiful spot, and she hadn't seen another soul all day. She turned her face to the water again as she walked, watching as the sky lit up into a symphony of purples, pinks and oranges as the sun began to dip toward the horizon. Without warning, she fell over something large on the ground, landing squarely on a warm, hard object, which gave a startled grunt.

She scrambled up as quickly as possible, but not before she pressed up against the length of a tall, muscular man. He was warm and smelled of the ocean and the wind—and also a bit spicy, like some of the more exotic seasonings used in the local dishes. As she brushed herself off and stood as swiftly as she could, she just had time to realize that he smelled…incredibly good. *For someone I apparently fell on like a ton of bricks. Smooth. Real smooth, Annelise.*

Home of Erotic Romance

Sign up for our newsletter and find out about all our romance book releases, eBook sales and promotions, sneak peeks and FREE romance books!

About the Author

Zelah Roberts grew up in a beautiful leafy market town in North East England. She spent a happy childhood exploring the surrounding woods and moorlands, and visiting ancient priories, abbeys, and roman ruins with her history-buff parents. These inspired her imagination, and many notebooks were filled with action-packed tales of adventure and romance.

An avid reader with eclectic tastes, her teenage years were spent navigating the magical worlds of Narnia and Middle Earth by way of Earthsea. As she grew older, her tastes expanded to take in thrillers and romance, and a degree in English introduced her to the great classics of literature.

After many jobs ranging from traffic warden to project manager, Zelah now divides her time between writing and teaching English and creative writing. When she is not lost in daydreams about her new book, she also loves spending time with her family, travelling and visiting the theatre and cinema.

Zelah loves to hear from readers. You can find her contact information, website details and author profile page at https://www.totallybound.com